MW01674351

Shattered Dreams

by S.M. Leblond

DORRANCE
PUBLISHING CO
EST. 1920
PITTSBURGH, PENNSYLVANIA 15238

Dorrance Publishing Co
585 Alpha Drive
Pittsburgh, PA 15238
Visit our website at *www.dorrancebookstore.com*

ISBN: 978-1-6366-1117-4
EISBN: 978-1-6495-7347-6

Shattered Dreams

Dedicated to Joann Grayson, who has never stopped believing in me, and has never given up on me.

I'd also like to thank Sue Weaver for inspiring me in high school to write. I got a little lost over the years but found my way back.

Most Importantly, I'd like to thank my parents. You were always there for me. Encouraging me to succeed in every aspect of my life. Most importantly for making sure that I graduated and got my high school diploma against all odds. You're the most amazing parents ever. Thank you for everything. From my heart to yours.

People who are having sex with children are not johns and tricks. They are child rapists and pedophiles. So, we should call them what they are.

- Jada Pinkett Smith

Our lives begin to end the day we become silent about things that matter.

- Rev. Martin Luther King Jr.

Our fight against human trafficking is one of the great human rights causes of our time.

- US President Barack Obama

Sex Trafficking can occur within street prostitution, brothels, homes, escort services, massage parlors, and other establishments posing as legitimate businesses.

-The A-21 Campaign

In approximately 46 percent of trafficking cases, the recruiter had a previous relationship established with the victim.

-The A-21 Campaign

The world is a dangerous place, not because of those who do evil, but because of those who look on and do nothing.

- Albert Einstein

It took me so long to find my voice. It took me too long to claim my life as my own and say no to all others who tried to steal it away and make it theirs. But I'm awake now and there is no going back to sleep.

— Beth Belleisle

Chapter 1

SEBASTIAN OPENS HIS EYES. HIS HEART POUNDS, HIS HEAD aches. As he tries to sit up, the room spins. Sebastian lies back down. Where is he? He tries again to sit up, tries looking around the room but that just makes things worse. The room spins faster, making him nauseous. He grabs his head as his body sinks back against the gurney. Sebastian slips into darkness.

Something's wrong. He can feel it. Every bone in his body aches. He tries to remember who he is, how he got wherever he is. His mind becomes groggy, black dots blur his vision. The darkness overtakes him. Tears cloud Sebastian's eyes. Sebastian's last thought before passing out, *Aidez moi! S'il vous Plait!Aidez moi!*

Dr. Adeel Maboob takes one look at the young man lying naked on the gurney. This boy is in more trouble than Luscious Corbett led him to believe. Dr. Maboob has been on Luscious Corbett's payroll for eight years. He has never seen one beaten this badly before. What had this young man done to deserve such a beating? This poor boy has lived through the worst kind of torment and torture. How is he still alive and breathing? How did this young man wind up in Luscious Corbett's servitude?

Dr. Maboob stitches up the young man's wounds, gives him a tetanus shot, and a pain reliever – a little more than necessary. This young man will need all the help he can get. Dr. Maboob covers the young man's frail body with a warm soft cotton blanket. He will have a long recovery ahead of him followed by a life of hell. Luscious Corbett will be wanting compensation for the young man's medical bills. He will face a lifetime of servitude. But first he must make it through the night.

Dr. Maboob has tried to help the men and women who have passed through his clinic over the past eight years. He's learned over time that no one cares. Money lines the pockets of the masters. Corbett is a powerful man, and no one will stand up against him. Dr. Maboob receives large monthly payments from Luscious Corbett for services rendered. Those payments are paying off Dr. Maboob's school loans in half the time. The law will prosecute him right along with the rest of Luscious Corbett's gang. He has seen and heard things that could get him killed if he ever repeated them. Dr. Maboob gives the indentured servants the best medical care possible in hopes that it will be enough to give them what they need to survive.

Sebastian opens his eyes. The pain in his head has subsided. The room is no longer spinning. Sebastian sits up. He is still on a medical gurney. He is covered with a soft warm cotton blanket. He's naked except for a clean pair of white briefs. There's an IV attached to his left arm. The IV's attached to a bag of saline with some kind of red liquid dripping into the saline bag. Sebastian realizes that the red liquid must be some kind of medicine that stops the room from spinning and subdue his aching head. Next to the bed on a small metal table is a plate with a cheese and turkey sandwich and a glass of milk.

"It's OK, eat. It's not drugged or poisoned. You're going to need all the energy and strength you can muster. I must return you to Monsieur Corbett tomorrow morning." Dr. Maboob sadly informs the young man.

Sebastian takes a bite of the sandwich and a large gulp of milk. He nervously eyes the doctor.

"Merci. Who are you? Where am I?"

"I'm Dr. Nairobi Adeel Maboob. You're a patient at my medical clinic. Monsieur Corbett and his men brought you here two days ago. Do you remember your name or what happened to you?

"Je m'appelle Sebastian. I'm an indentured servant at Monsieur Corbett's Chalet. I owe him a rather large debt. Until my debt is paid, he owns my life. The debt never gets any smaller. We are charged room and board. Monsieur Corbett also charges us for the food and beverages we consume. He will charge me for whatever medical care you have provided me. I'll never be able to pay it off. The wounds you treated, I received as a punishment. I know you can't help me any more than you already have, so thank you for saving what's left of my life. I've heard of you, the indentured servants back at the Chalet say you will mail letters. Is this true?"

"Oui, but you must be careful. I read the letters before mailing them. If there's anything in the letters that can trace back to me or give any idea as to how to find you I'm afraid that I would be forced to destroy those letters. You see I know too much. Like you, I'm in too deep. Keep it simple and I'll mail them. I cross into Belgium once a month. I mail the letters while I'm there. I visit Monsieur Corbett's Chalet at the beginning and the middle of each month. My car has tinted windows. I leave the back left window cracked. Place your letter in an unsealed, self-addressed stamped envelope. Drop it through the window and walk away. No return address. I'll help you but only if you help yourself. Now lie down and get some rest. Monsieur Corbett will be here early in the morning to pick you up and take you back to the Chalet. I'm sorry I did the best I could. I hope it's enough." Dr. Maboob explains as he exits the room.

Sebastian eats the rest of the sandwich and gulps down the rest of the milk. He looks around the room. There are no windows. No way out. Dr. Maboob locked the door on his way out. Sebastian's best option is to rest. His day will start early tomorrow morning. Exhausted, he lies back and closes his eyes. The short conversation with the doctor left him feeling exhausted. Sleep comes quickly.

Sebastian opens his eyes and stares at the clock on the wall, 0500. He stares at the clock wishing for a few more hours. Dr. Maboob stands next to his gurney. He hands Sebastian two egg and cheese croissants, a tall glass of juice, and a tablet for pain.

"Eat and drink quickly. Monsieur Corbett has called from the chalet. His men will be here in 20 minutes. I'm sorry. I wish there was more I could have done for you."

"Merci, I know you did what you could. They'll restrain me for transport. Please don't watch. Just makes it more humiliating." Sebastian drops his gaze to the floor embarrassed.

Dr. Maboob hands Sebastian a clean pair of jeans, a clean shirt, white socks, and his shoes. Sebastian slowly dresses while eating his breakfast. He swallows the pain tablet.

Monsieur Corbett's men arrive at the medical clinic. Sebastian gets to his feet, turns, and faces the wall. He painfully drops to his knees, crosses his ankles, and places his hands behind his back. He waits for the flex cuffs. Sebastian knows it'll go easier if he doesn't fight it. That lesson, he has learned. He won't make that mistake again. He will find a way to pleasure the male clients. He isn't ready to die, not yet.

Sebastian quickly and quietly leaves the medical clinic. Restrained, his head down, eyes on the floor he slowly walks out to the awaiting van. Corbett's men roughly shove Sebastian into the back of the white paneled van parked in the back alley. He sits where he can see both men. Sits where he can see if a strike is coming. The two goons won't touch him. Monsieur Corbett wants him back in one piece. They won't go against a direct order. Upon his return Sebastian will be stripped and his body searched for new wounds.

Twenty minutes later the van pulls up to the Chalet's gates, honks the horn twice and waits for the gates to open before pulling around to the backside of the Chalet. The door violently slides open and Sebastian is dragged out of the van. He is forced to march across the gravel and through the backdoor into the Chalet's back kitchen. He is harshly pushed down onto his knees. Sebastian lowers his head and eyes. He stares at the floor. He waits quietly.

"Aucun probleme?" Luscious Corbett asks the two men.

"Non, Monsieur, he came quietly." Luc answers.

"Enlever ses reticent." Corbett instructs Francois.

Francois walks over and pulls out his knife. He cuts away Sebastian's restraints. Sebastian lets his arms fall to his side. He wants to rub his arms and wrists but refuses to show any sign of weakness in front of his master.

Corbett stares at Sebastian, "levez-vous, bande, tour."

Sebastian shakily stands up, removes his clothing, and turns slowly in a circle. Keeping his head down and his arms by his sides. If he attempts to cover any part of his body he will be whipped. Sebastian waits for further instructions.

Luscious Corbett walks a slow circle around Sebastian, dismisses Luc and Francois. Sebastian shivers as Corbett stares at his naked body. He remains silent with his head down. Corbett asks no questions as he hands Sebastian his clothing and motions for him to quickly dress.

"My mother was an American student touring Europe when she met my father. My father was born and raised here in Paris. He fell in love with my mother at first sight. My father was a businessman. He ran a small firm that provided models to the local television studios. My father married my mother and the two of them built they're small firm into an international empire. After my mother passed away, I stepped up and helped my father with his firm. He taught me all his secrets including training models here at the Chalet. He picked up the side business of private offerings to entertain his wealthy clientele. What a client wants, a client gets. Do you understand, Sebastian?"

"Oui, Monsieur." Sebastian quickly answers.

"Clients don't like their offerings to be marked up, or in your case stitched up. So until your wounds have properly healed you will be working here in the kitchens. You will prepare meals, wash dishes, sweep, mop, clean the restrooms, and in general remain silent and invisible. You will be bedding down in the small room at the back of the kitchen. Your bunkmate brought your things up last night. We are eating breakfast now so you may eat a small portion of food. It will help with keeping your strength up. You will begin with washing the dishes. You will eat your meals after the main house guests have all been served.

You will wash dishes, sweep, mop, and prep for the next meal. At the end of the day you may bunk down after all your nightly chores have been completed. Your restroom is to be cleaned and scrubbed daily. You will get up at four thirty in the morning and start prepping for breakfast. There's a small bathroom just to the left of your quarters that you may use for all your personal hygiene needs. You have ten minutes to get settled into your new quarters, eat breakfast, and start your chores. Do you understand, Sebastian?"

"Oui, Monsieur."

Sebastian looks around his new living quarters. The room is half the size he's used to but at least it's clean and has a door. The bathroom is small making it easier to keep it clean. There is a shower, a sink, and a toilet. Having already eaten breakfast at the clinic, he immediately starts washing dishes. Sebastian has washed dishes before. He had worked in the kitchen at the orphanage where he'd grown up and lived until almost a year ago. His debts had piled up before he had come to Monsieur Corbett for a loan. Unable to pay his loan back in the time allotted, he had been forced to sign a contract and move into Monsieur Corbett's Chalet as an indentured servant. It was explained that he would only have to stay at the Chalet and live in the servant's quarters until his debt was paid off. The longer he stayed, the larger his debt became. Sebastian quickly learned that almost everyone working at the chalet was an indentured servant. Room and board, as well as the cost of food and beverages, and any medical bills they accumulated while living at the compound were automatically deducted from their wages. Once his fees and services are taken out, he still has to pay for laundry and hygiene needs. He's allowed to shop in the small gift shop on the grounds for all his needs. He also has a clothing allowance that is taken from his salary as well. The Chalet provides him and the other servants with a seven-day supply of clothing. Men do their laundry on Sundays and the women on Mondays. In the end, there's little to no physical pay for services rendered.

My Dearest Kindle,

I have made terrible mistakes and must learn from them before I'm allowed to return home. The people here are nice and provide me with the things I need to live. I work hard to pay off my debts and hope to make a difference in the person I wish to become. It will take some time to pay off my debts, just know that I love you and miss you.

Kindle, you shouldn't have to pay for my mistakes. Finish University and be the best that you can be. Please don't make the same mistakes I've made: don't borrow what you cannot pay back. You're smarter than that. Tell your parents I miss them.

When I sink into the water there is no pain, no humiliation. Just peace and silence, I think mostly of you and how to make all this right one day.

There is so much pain and anger in the world, how do we survive? How do we overcome all the pain, all the anger, all the humiliation?

Love,
Sebastian

Chapter 2

SEBASTIAN KEEPS HIS HEAD DOWN AND WORKS HARD FOR 16 excruciating days, 12 to 18 hours a day. Dr. Maboob arrives at the Chalet to check in on Sebastian 10 days after his return to the Chalet and declares that he is physically fit and healthy enough to resume his service.

Sebastian hands Dr. Maboob his first letter, "Nothing in the letter should cause any trouble, nothing in it hints at where I am. Merci, doctor; she's important to me." Sebastian gets up and walks out of the room. He returns to the kitchen to prepare this evening's dinner. Dr. Maboob puts Sebastian's letter in his bag, reports to Luscious Corbett that Sebastian is fully recovered and ready to return to work. He knows that Sebastian was forced to return to work the same day he returned to the Chalet. It was refreshing not to see any new wounds or marks on Sebastian's body. Luscious Corbett keeps Sebastian working in the kitchen for six more long, excruciating days after the doctor's visit. Luscious forces him to scrub the floors and baseboards as well as the walls. Sebastian polishes every piece of stainless steel in the kitchen.

Sebastian is happy when he's told that he may return to the small room in the servant's quarters where he shares a room with another young man. Sergei, his bunkmate, has been indentured to Monsieur

Corbett for two years. Sergei's trying to pay off his father's gambling debts. His father is in a wheelchair and unable to pay off his own debts. Sergei is 16, two years younger than Sebastian. They have been bunking together because of their closeness in age. Most of the other male servants living and working at the Chalet are in their 20's. The female servants range in age from 16 to their early to mid-twenties.

Sergei's relieved to have his roommate back. He helps Sebastian unpack his few belongings and set up his side of the room again.

"What happened? Why were you taken away? Where did you go?" Sergei asks.

"I was called to Monsieur Corbett's office. I was told to deliver the two american females, Candice and Rebecca, to Mr. Ryan's private suite on the third floor. Only Mr. Ryan wasn't interested in the two young ladies; he was more interested in me. I tried to explain to him that I wasn't intended as an offering. Candice and Rebecca were his intended offerings. He became insistent, pushed Candice and Rebecca out of the room and instructed me to remove my clothing and to present myself. I've never been with a man before. I've always been presented as an offering to female clientele. I refused to undress and present myself to Mr. Ryan. That angered Mr. Ryan so he called Monsieur Corbett's private line and complained that I was refusing to follow his instructions.

Monsieur Corbett came upstairs and harshly instructed me to follow Mr. Ryan's instructions to the letter or face the consequences for breach of contract. I was to do whatever Mr. Ryan asked of me. I removed my clothing and stood with my hands at my side. I started shaking from head to toe. I just couldn't do it. I grabbed my clothing and ran. I made it to the stables. I was getting dressed when Francois and Luc showed up, you know, Monsieur Corbett's brainless muscle men. They attacked me and forced me onto my knees. Luc grabbed a fistful of my hair and punched me in the face several times. Francois kicked me and whipped me with a leather whip. The beating lasted so long that I eventually passed out in a pool of my own blood. I awoke two days later at Dr. Maboob's medical clinic. The doc had stitched me up and put me back together. I stayed at the clinic until Luc and Francois returned and brought me back to the Chalet. Upon my return to the compound, I was greeted and inspected by Monsieur Corbett. I was reminded of my place on the almighty totem pole. I've been working in the kitchen for the past 16 days scrubbing, cleaning, and shining every surface, wall, baseboard, and floor. When I wasn't scrubbing every surface in the kitchen I was setting up and preparing meals. Each day ended and another began." Sebastian angrily informs Sergei.

"I'm sorry, Sebastian, it should have been me. I know what the male clientele expect. I know how to pleasure them. It's nothing new to me."

"How do you do it? I mean at some point it must have been your first time. How did you know what to do?" Sebastian asks.

"The first time, I was scared to death. My father's business partner hit on me. He was older, more sophisticated than I. I was only 12 at the time. My father's business partner was in his mid to late thirties. More than half my age. I had gone to my father's office to visit him. I was waiting alone in his office. My father was down the hall taking a conference call when his business partner entered the office looking for my father. He commented on what a handsome young man I was growing into. He came over and sat down next to me. He offered me a shot of whiskey. One whiskey became two, became something like five or six. He removed my clothing and taught me the ways of a man. When it was all over and done with, I left the office and ran home crying. I hid in my room all night. But something stirred inside me after that day. I never told my mother or father what had happened that day. A year later while away at summer camp I experimented with a boy closer to my age, but again more experienced. I could teach you as he taught me. If you think it would help?"

Sebastian thinks about Sergei's story as well as his offer while getting ready for bed that night. He crawls into bed and glances over to Sergei's side of the room. Sergei hasn't shut off his bedside lamp. Tomorrow's Sunday, most likely they would only have lightweight house chores to do. Most clients leave Sunday morning and head back to their everyday lives. Next week's clients weren't due to arrive until Monday afternoon. Tomorrow's workload will be light. They're given an extra hour of sleep on Sundays. Religious services are by choice and mostly watched on the tele. Most have given up on any belief in God by the end of their first year at the Chalet. They either bury themselves in religion to cope with the pain and humiliation or turn their backs on it completely. Neither Sergei nor Sebastian cared much for religion. Most religions wouldn't accept their lifestyles anyway. No matter if it wasn't their lifestyle by choice, but rather a lifestyle forced upon them.

"Sergei, are you tired?" Sebastian nervously asks.

"I'm awake, what's up?" Sergei has an idea of what's on his roommate's mind, what he wants to talk about by the way he is uncomfortably fidgeting and trying to sit up in his bed.

Sebastian clears his throat a few times, leans his back against the cool cinder block wall. "I was just wondering if you felt like talking a little?" Sebastian asks.

"Sure, tomorrow's Sunday. I wasn't planning on going to bed for another hour or two. The lady clients from Hong Kong left earlier today. There won't be any late night offerings tonight."

"Yeah, about that, kind of wanted to talk about that a little. Offerings I mean. You know when you're offered up as an offering to male clients." Sebastian nervously stumbles.

"Where do you want to start? At the beginning?"

"Yeah, how did you first deal with it? I mean, how did you get through it?" Sebastian asks.

"At first it was hard. I was just a confused kid. I explained to the boy at the camp that I had never done it before. I never counted the drunken rape as being real. I couldn't process or remember much about it anyway so I buried it deep within me, never to see the light of day again. Only the memory of uncomfortable pain lingered. He taught me to focus on something calming in the room, concentrate even when it wasn't there to be seen. Picture it in my head. The second thing he taught me was to use scented candles or scented oils to get past the smell of men and the alcohol they drank. When I was in the fifth grade, I had this hot teacher. She always smelled of peppermint. So, I bought a few bottles of peppermint oil when I first arrived at the Chalet. You can borrow a bottle if you like. I buy it in the gift shop, next to the scented candles and potpourris. Anyway, when Monsieur Corbett informs me that I'll be entertaining male clientele I put some of the oil on my hands and arms, not the chest though it's too strong. I keep a small bottle in the pockets of my robes. I concentrate on the peppermint oil. For me, it's gotten easier over time. Some men are anything but sexy, much less attractive. Sometimes you have to take a mini vacation in your head. Totally, mentally remove yourself from your surroundings. I picture myself on a cruise with my fifth grade primary teacher. Then comes practice. You have to find someone willing to be gentle and slow. Rape isn't going to teach you anything except pain, misery and humiliation. So, how do you want to proceed? There is only so much I can talk you through. Physical experimentation is a lesson best learned in private with someone you trust."

Sebastian thinks hard about what Sergei is offering to do. His heart pounds, the room begins spinning. Sebastian takes a few deep breaths. He slowly gets out of bed and removes his clothing. He quickly steps over his clothing lying on the floor and climbs under the covers of Sergei's bed.

"Remember, slow and gentle. I might pass out on you or worse humiliate myself by puking all over myself or worse all over you."

Sergei sits up and positions himself, straddling Sebastian's chest he opens a bottle of peppermint oil and slowly caresses it onto Sebastian's arms. Sebastian closes his eyes and deeply inhales the scent of peppermint oil as Sergei hands gently caresses the oil into his skin.

Chapter 3

SEBASTIAN RESTLESSLY STARES UP AT THE CEILING. THE ROOM looks different. It takes him a few seconds to realize that his and Sergei's beds have been pushed together. That it is Sergei's arm wrapped around his chest. The soft scent of peppermint floods his memory. Sergei pushes himself up on one arm. He smiles and brushes Sebastian's hair out of his face.

"Good morning, how are you feeling this morning?"

The room begins spinning. Sebastian feels a sharp pain in his stomach. "Don't judge me or think any less of me." Sebastian groans as he jumps out of bed and rushes into the bathroom where he proceeds to violently vomit for a good 10 minutes.

Sergei waits until Sebastian's finished, he walks to the bathroom and leans against the door frame. "I'm sorry I know it's a bit overwhelming the first few times. It'll pass, get easier with time. I promise. I thought you handled it pretty well for your first time."

Sebastian leans back against the cold cinderblock wall, wipes his mouth on the back of his hand and stares at the floor.

"I'm sorry. There's this girl back home waiting for me. Only I'll probably never see her again. This is my life now and there is no escaping it. I messed up bad and there's no going back." Sebastian catches his breath as tears fill his eyes. He hugs the porcelain pot and hurls again.

Sergei walks back to his bed and sits down. He waits. Right now, Sebastian needs privacy. Sergei hears the shower turn on. He walks down to the servant's dining room and puts together two breakfast plates. Sergei walks back to his and Sebastian's room and waits patiently for the shower to turn off.

"You OK?" Sergei asks as he hands Sebastian his breakfast plate.

"All's Good. Merci, you won't tell anyone?" Sebastian nervously asks as he reaches for the plate of food.

"Never" Sergei replies.

Sergei and Sebastian eat in silence. Afterwards they push the two beds back against their respective walls on opposite sides of their tiny room.

"What are your plans for today?" Sergei asks Sebastian.

"GPS wrist monitor." Sebastian answers.

"What?" Sergei looks confused.

"Monsieur Corbett has a VIP Client flying in. He has instructed me that I will be accompanying him to the airport today."

"Oh, everything alright? You look a bit nervous? You're not going to hurl again are you?"

"No. Except for being lectured or reprimanded, I have never been alone with Monsieur Corbett. Personally, I don't really like him and I'm pretty sure the feelings are mutual. I'm just wondering how I'm supposed to act once we're alone together in the car." Sebastian tells Sergei as he dresses in a dark suit and tie. Monsieur Corbett had given it to him the night before. He had called Sebastian to his office Saturday evening to inform him that his punishment was over and that he would be returning to his room in the servants quarters.

"How long of a ride is it to the airport?" Sergei asks.

"I don't know. I was a young kid about seven or eight the last time I went to the airport. An hour, maybe two. Depending on the traffic."

Sebastian freezes. Monsieur Corbett's heavy footsteps walk down the hallway towards their living quarters. "Best of luck Sebastian, it's my turn to serve lunch today in the servant's quarters. Good day, Monsieur Corbett." Sergei addresses his master as he walks past him and heads down the hall towards the servant's dining room.

Luscious Corbett enters Sebastian's and Sergei's small quarters. He looks around the room. Sebastian stands next to his bed at attention arms by his side.

"Relax; I'm not here to torture or humiliate you. The young man leaving he's your flat mate?"

"Oui, Monsieur"

"Relax you're not in trouble. You may speak English today. The client we're meeting at the airport speaks primarily English. You will make him feel welcomed. You and your roommate keep a clean flat that reflects well upon you both." Monsieur Corbett informs Sebastian.

"Merci."

Luscious Corbett pulls out a GPS wrist monitor from the inside pocket of his suit and instructs Sebastian to take a seat, hold up his left arm and pull up his shirt sleeve. Sebastian takes a seat in one of the two chairs at the small round table in the corner of the room next to the dish sink and small counter. He holds up his left arm and pulls up his shirt sleeve. Luscious Corbett attaches the black GPS wrist monitor to Sebastian's left wrist and instructs him to drop his left arm and stand up.

"Sebastian, have you ever driven a Bentley Continental?

"Non, Monsieur. I mostly drove the old vehicles owned by the orphanage around Paris when it was my turn to pick the other kids up from their different school activities."

"Today, you will be acting as my private chauffeur. If all goes well, you will be acting as Dr. Robert's private chauffeur for the week. You shouldn't have any problems. The Bentley Continental comes equipped with built in GPS." Monsieur Corbett explains as he and Sebastian walk to the garage together. Sebastian walks two steps behind Luscious Corbett.

As Sebastian gets into the Bentley, he realizes that it still has that leather new car smell. The car is sleek and sexy, the inside leather matches the black of the car's exterior.

Monsieur Corbett hands Sebastian the remote key and instructs him to stick it in his pocket and keep it with him at all times. Sebastian does as he is instructed and presses the button that starts the car's engine. The car roars to life. Once running it purrs like a kitten. Sebastian shifts the car into reverse and slowly backs the Bentley out of the garage.

"Sebastian, we're going to be in the car together for an hour or two, what should we discuss?" Luscious Corbett taunts Sebastian.

"Whatever Monsieur wishes." Sebastian nervously answers.

"You've never pleasured the same sex before, have you?" Luscious gets right to the point.

Sebastian's heart races. He takes a deep breath to steady himself. "Non, Monsieur. Again, I'm sorry. The client is to be given whatever his or her desires are." Sebastian recites the oath.

"Dr. Roberts is a sexual behavior therapist, maybe you should talk with him this week about your sexual discomforts and performance issues." Luscious Corbett suggests.

"Oui, Monsieur."

"How long have you been with us at the Chalet?"

"A little over a year, Monsieur."

"Sebastian, how old are you?"

"Eighteen."

"Were you sexually active before arriving at my Chalet?"

"No, I was a virgin."

"Your first sexual encounters were with Cinnamon than during your training? Had you ever watched pornography before arriving at the Chalet?"

"No, not before my training."

"So, you really were a virgin, a rookie when you arrived? How do you feel about sex now?"

Sebastian thinks about this for a moment. "Honestly, it terrifies me."

Luscious smiles and laughs "All of it, or just the thought of having to pleasure a man?"

"All of it, Monsieur."

"Good, I wouldn't have believed you if you had answered any differently. You're honest, that's important. How will you handle it the next time a man hits on you, or turns away his offerings and expects you to be his offering instead?"

Sebastian thinks about his master's question. Should he tell him about Sergei and they're experimenting? It would be the honest thing to do. Corbett appreciated his honesty so far. Sebastian takes a deep calming breath. He steadies himself.

"Monsieur Corbett I'm going to be honest with you because you seem to appreciate honesty. Sergei, my bunkmate has been coaching me on how to be more pleasurable with male clientele. We experimented with male pleasuring last night." Sebastian nervously answers.

"I appreciate your honesty and applaud you for your bravery to try new things. That will take you far in life. So how did your little experiment go?"

Sebastian gives this question a lot of thought. "Honestly, it was awkward, humiliating, and most of all painful. I woke up this morning and vomited for 10 minutes. But I learned that I'm stronger than I give myself credit. I can only hope that any future male clients will be as gentle and patient with me as Sergei was last night."

Luscious Corbett looks pleased. "Dr. Roberts can help you with your problems. I'm sure he would be willing to work with you on a more one on one basis while you act as his chauffeur this week."

Luscious turns the radio on and listens to beautiful classical orchestra music for the rest of their journey to the airport giving Sebastian time to think about their conversation.

Sergei knows he's in trouble the minute he steps into the office, Luc the good-looking dumb gorilla is standing behind the desk, there's a thick leather strap sitting out on the desk. Luc is Monsieur Corbett's son. Luc's left in charge when Monsieur Corbett is away from the chalet. The second dumb ugly gorilla Francois is standing beside him. Francois is Monsieur Corbett's nephew and second in command when Corbett's away.

Sergei shakes as he enters the room, he walks to the center of the room and stands at attention. Francois walks around Sergei and closes the office door behind him. Francois returns to the front of the desk, picks up the thick leather strap. Francois stares evilly at Sergei. Sergei had been five minutes late reporting to the servant's kitchen this morning. He had served yesterday's cold leftovers from the main guest house kitchens to his fellow servants. Five lashes, one for each minute that he was late. That Sergei can handle. It's the remaining lashes for the dropped pan of crepes on the floor that will cost him dearly.

He'd been shocked to see the two dumb gorillas in the kitchen this morning. Normally, they ate all their meals up at the main guest house dining facilities. A much nicer dining room that's reserved for the Chalet's guests. I guess with Corbett away they had decided to take their bad moods out on the indentured servants. They had whipped Jade earlier this morning in the kitchen for washing dishes too slow. Sergei had been left to finish the dishes by himself. He had washed as fast as he could knowing that he was to report to the main office as soon as he was finished.

"Assume the position Sergei." Luc orders.

Sergei unbuttons his shirt and removes it; he lowers himself onto his knees and crosses his ankles. Sergei intertwines his fingers behind his head, takes a deep breath and makes eye contact with Luc. Francois positions himself behind Sergei.

"Five strokes, one for each minute that you were late this morning. Five strokes for dropping food on the floor and 10 more strokes for wasting food. Do you have anything to say in your defense before your punishment is carried out?" Luc asks.

It's a trick question. If you say anything in your own defense, the strokes are doubled. Just out of pure spite.

Sergei looks at Luc and answers." Non, Monsieur."

The first stroke of the leather strap lands squarely across the middle of his back taking his breath away. The second almost knocks him on the floor. By the fourth he can no longer handle the pain; Sergei cries out. He fights with every ounce of bravery not to fall to the floor. Any sign of weakness will incur ridicule and more lashes. After 20 lashes Sergei is shaking and unable to stand up on his own.

Luc walks around the desk, picks up his shirt and tosses it into Sergei's face. Luc informs him that he has 5 minutes to clean up and compose himself. He's to report to the stables for the rest of the day he will be mucking out the stalls.

Francois lays the leather strap on the desk and follows Luc out of the office.

Chapter 4

SEBASTIAN PULLS UP TO THE AIRPORT TERMINAL AND PARKS IN line with the rest of the limos and taxis. Luscious Corbett instructs Sebastian to stay with the car and await his and Dr. Roberts' return. Sebastian locks the car and stands next to the Bentley awaiting Monsieur Corbett and Dr. Roberts' return. Sebastian eyes the other chauffeurs out of the corner of his eye. Monsieur Corbett hadn't given him any instructions as to what he was supposed to do while he awaited their return. Some of the chauffeurs held decorative placards with the name of the client they were picking up, others spit on a white rag and wiped away imaginary spots of dirt that were supposed to be on their cars. Yet others looking very serious talked on cell phones and others like him stood next to their cars like guard dogs. Sebastian looks for any sign of dirt on the car. The Bentleys are washed daily by his fellow servants for the use of the clientele staying at the Chalet needing to be chauffeured around Paris. Upon finding no dirt to wipe away, he stands duty-bound next to the Bentley, awaiting Monsieur Corbett's return. Sebastian notices that several of the chauffeurs run to the door as soon as they see they're car's owner returning. These chauffeurs take their guest's luggage and briefcases from their guests before running back to their respective cars. They place the luggage in the trunk of the car and place the briefcases on the floor standing up in the back of the car as soon as they open the car door for their boss or guest. Sebastian decides that upon seeing Monsieur Corbett and Dr. Roberts returning to the car he will briskly walk to the doors and relieve them of Dr. Roberts' luggage and briefcase. Twenty minutes pass before Sebastian eyes Monsieur Corbett and another gentleman walking across the large airport foyer's entrance. He briskly walks to greet Monsieur Corbett and Dr. Roberts at the doors. He opens the door, relieves Dr. Roberts of his suitcase and dress bag as well as his briefcase. The suitcase has wheels, but none of the other chauffeurs had rolled the luggage. They had all carried the suitcases with the dress bags draped neatly over their arms, briefcases in their other hand. Sebastian briskly walks back to the Bentley and pops the trunk. He lays the suitcase in the trunk first and drapes the dress bag across the top of the large suitcase careful not to wrinkle the clothing inside as the other chauffeurs had done for the past 20 minutes. He closes the trunk and walks around to the side of the car. Sebastian opens the right rear door and places the briefcase on the floor of the car standing up. He greets Dr. Roberts as he helps him into the car before running to the other side of the car and opening the left rear door to assist his boss into the rear of the car joining Dr. Roberts for the ride back to the Chalet. He then walks briskly around the front of the Bentley and takes a seat in the driver's seat.

"Sebastian, the Chalet s'il vous plait." Luscious Corbett instructs.

"Oui, Monsieur."

Corbett raises the partition between the driver and his guest. Sebastian hits a few buttons on the GPS and pulls away from the airport. The drive back to the resort is relaxing. He finds himself getting comfortable with his new duties as a chauffeur and personal assistant to the American doctor. The music relaxes him, and he begins to enjoy the drive back.

Sebastian pulls up to the Chalet's gates and honks the horn twice. The gates open and he pulls through. He drives the car around the circular drive to the front doors of the large manor house, stops the car and turns it off. He exits the car and opens Dr. Roberts' door for him. Sebastian walks around to the other side of the car popping the trunk as he passes by and opens Monsieur Corbett's door before returning to the trunk and pulling Dr. Roberts' luggage and dress bag out of the trunk. Sebastian follows Monsieur Corbett and Dr. Roberts two steps behind up the walkway to the main guest house. He follows two steps behind all the way to Dr. Roberts' private suite on the third floor.

After laying the suitcase on the luggage rack next to the bed and hanging the dress bag in the closet Sebastian asks permission to excuse himself.

"Sebastian, you are to return the Bentley to the garage. You will wash, wax, and detail the car. Vacuum and deodorize the interior before returning to my office. Do you understand?" Luscious Corbett instructs Sebastian.

"Oui, Monsieur."

Sebastian drives the Bentley slowly back to the garage and spends the next hour washing, waxing and detailing the Bentley inside and out. He locks the car up, returns the remote key to the key box, and heads back towards the main guest house to Monsieur Corbett's office. On his way back towards the main guest house Sebastian notices Sergei walking slowly in what looks like a great deal of pain across the grounds. Sergei is heading towards the servant's quarters. Sebastian calls out to Sergei. Sergei turns, the pain and discomfort registering on his rugged, handsome face worries Sebastian. He wants to go over and talk with him but he is expected in Monsieur Corbett's office. Sebastian waves. Sergei raises his arm to wave back and winces in pain. Sergei turns and heads back towards their living quarters. Concerned Sebastian wants to follow him but instead fearing punishment, he heads straight to Monsieur Corbett's office. Sebastian enters through the side servant's entrance and walks to his master's office. When he arrives at the door to Corbett's office, there's a heated conversation going on between Monsieur Corbett and his two lieutenants. Sebastian takes a deep breath and knocks on the door.

“Entrer” Monsieur Corbett angrily answers.

Sebastian hesitantly opens the door and steps through. Just as he prepares to close the door Luscious Corbett instructs him to leave the door open.

“Luc and Francois were just leaving. Would you be so kind as to close the door behind them as they exit my office. I’m not sure either one of these two buffoons would know proper etiquette if it hit them on their arse on their way out the door.” Luscious instructs Sebastian.

“Oui, Monsieur.”

Sebastian enjoys Luc and Francois’ uncomfortable exit from the room with their tails tucked firmly between their legs. He wants nothing more than to smirk at them but knows he would pay dearly for it in the end. For a second, he almost thinks it might be worth it. Remembering his last beating, Sebastian quickly changes his mind and suppresses the urge. He closes the door behind Luc and Francois, turns and walks to the center of the room. Sebastian stands with his arms straight by his sides. For the first time he notices the leather strap sitting on his master’s desk and wonders if it’s meant for him. Has he done something to displease his master?

Had it been meant for Luc and Francois? Even Luc and Francois received occasional punishments.

Luscious stares at Sebastian and catches him staring at the thick leather strap sitting on his desk. Luscious picks the leather strap up off his desk and places it in his top desk drawer. “Not today Sebastian, you did well.” Sebastian breaths a little easier. The strap wasn’t intended for him.

Luscious Corbett walks over to the mini bar in the corner by the window overlooking the stretch of grounds between the main guest house and the servant’s quarters. He pours himself a brandy and turns to stare at Sebastian.

“I’m afraid that the leather strap was used earlier today on your bunkmate, he will probably be in need of some aloe this evening.” Luscious informs Sebastian.

Sebastian remembers the heated conversation he had walked in on just moments ago. Sebastian remains quite unsure if he's supposed to speak.

Luscious turns back towards the mini bar and pours a second smaller glass of brandy. "Would you care for a drink?" Luscious offers Sebastian the glass. Sebastian wants to accept the glass but wonders if it's a trap. After a second he reaches out and accepts the brandy. He holds the glass and swirls the liquid.

"Drink up, you won't be punished. Have you ever had alcohol before?"

"Oui Monsieur." Sebastian swallows the brandy. It tastes great. He lowers the glass and watches as Corbett walks back to his desk and sits down. Corbett always stands behind or in front of his desk when he is planning to lecture or yell. Sebastian loosens his grip on the glass and relaxes.

"Sebastian, you handled yourself professionally today. There was no frenzy in your demeanor or panic in your eyes. You handled your chauffeur duties professionally. Your behavior has earned you and your bunkmate the night off. I'm afraid your bunkmate will be in need of rest and your medical services tonight.

Starting tomorrow morning at 0730 you will be chauffeuring Dr. Roberts around Paris for the next five days. Just a warning if you jack rabbit or endanger the Chalet in anyway, Luc and Francois will have no problem handling you and your bunkmate. You both will wish for a quick death; it will be unlike any pain you have ever known before. Do you understand?"

"Oui, Monsieur."

"Dr. Roberts is a close and personal friend of mine. Do not disappoint him or me in any way. You are to have the Bentley ready to leave by 0720. You're to be standing outside the guest house next to the car ready to receive his bags for the day. Do you understand?"

"Oui, Monsieur."

"One last thing Sebastian, Dr. Roberts speaks primarily American English. When spoken to or asked a question, answer only in English. You may leave your glass on the mini bar on your way out. You're dismissed."

"Oui, Monsieur. Merci."

Sebastian walks to the minibar and sets his glass down; he turns and silently leaves Monsieur Corbett's office. Sebastian walks across the main foyer and lets himself out. Once outside he quickened his pace across the yard towards the servant's quarters. He finds Sergei lying flat on his stomach in bed, angry red welts across his back. Sebastian is angered and sickened by the sight of his bunkmates' pain and humiliation. He turns and walks into the bathroom, pulls down the bottle of aloe lotion and returns to Sergei's bedside. He gingerly sits next to him on the bed and opens the bottle of lotion. "Should I rub it into my hands first to warm it up or will it feel better cold straight out of the bottle?"

Sergei turns his head and looks at Sebastian.

"Cold s' il vous plait, merci," Sergei chokes out. The pain still registering across his face, rage in his eyes.

Sebastian squirts the cold aloe lotion straight onto Sergei's back and gently rubs it in. Leaving a nice thick layer sitting on his skin. Sebastian can still feel the heat radiating off Sergei's back.

"If it makes you feel any better, I heard Monsieur Corbett lecturing Francois and Luc in a rather loud voice. He called them buffoons. They left his office silently with their tails tucked firmly between their legs. Do you want to tell me what happened?"

"I was five minutes late to work this morning. Five lashes. I dropped a pan of crepes on the floor, five more lashes. Ten more lashes were added for wasting food. I showed weakness by crying out. After 20 lashes I was only given five minutes to clean up and return to work. I put my shirt back on after running it under a cold water tap and reported to the stables where I mucked out the stalls all day. No food. No water. No breaks. Just backbreaking work." Sergei angrily informs Sebastian.

Sebastian walks back over to the bathroom and pulls out a hand towel and runs it under cold water before returning to Sergei's bedside and draping the towel across his back.

"It's starting to feel better, Merci."

"You're lying. I can still read the pain in your eyes. Are you hungry? You think you could eat? I'll walk down and get both of us a plate and some milk."

"Yeah, I'm starving. Make sure it's something I can eat lying down." Sergei smiles a genuine smile this time.

"Got it, a sandwich and a glass of milk. No problem."

Sebastian returns a short while later with two plates of cold roast beef and cheese sandwiches and two glasses of milk. Sergei's glass has a straw in it to make it easier for him to sip his milk through. Sergei rolls onto his side and tries to sit up, he winces in pain as the towel slides off his back. Sebastian and Sergei eat in silence.

Sebastian cleans up after their small meal and offers to help Sergei take a cold shower. Sergei is exhausted and falls asleep before Sebastian returns from the dining hall. Sebastian turns off the overhead light and turns on his small desk lamp clamped to his headboard. He takes a shower and runs cold water over the hand towel again before replacing it across Sergei's back. Sergei mumbles thanks in his sleep and starts snoring. Sebastian wakes up several times in the night to find Sergei moaning in pain. He puts more aloe on his back and runs the hand towel under cold water before replacing it across Sergei's back. In the morning he quietly moves around the room. Sergei won't have to be up for another hour. He quietly slips out and heads down to the garage. Sebastian retrieves the remote key from the key box, inspects the car and wipes it down once more before driving it up to the Main Guest House at 0720.

My Dearest Kindle,

I have been taught the lesson of humility and it's a lesson well learned. One that I will not soon forget. I'm working this week as a chauffeur and personal assistant to an American doctor. He is a kind man and treats me well. I have begun to work towards the man I want to become and to move away from the angry childish man I am or was. I have learned there are consequences for my actions, that not only affect me, but those around me as well.

The pain and humiliation teach, as well as shames me. I hope to walk away with fewer scars and more patience. I have carried a chip on my shoulder for far too long. I have no idea who I am or where I came from. I have no memory of my parents, only memories of the orphanage. I'm angered by my mind's weakness, angered by the empty hollowness that is always present. I have only small amounts of trust and even smaller amounts of patience or love. I only remember ever loving you. I trusted your parents, but it's not the same. Does that make sense?

I hope to become a stronger, better, man; the kind of man you deserve. My bunkmate Sergei is 16, he should be home reading poetry or watching horror flicks... He's supposed to be a rebellious teen in general, but instead he is forced to pay his father's debts. I never want to be that kind of father. My children will never have to pay for my mistakes. I know you don't understand what any of this means. Please don't try to figure any of it out. It'll just give you a headache. Just know I'm alive and well.

I miss and love you dearly,
Sebastian

Chapter 5

SEBASTIAN STARES AT THE BRIGHT YELLOW LETTER BOX ACROSS the street. He addresses the envelope and affixes the correct postage. Dr. Roberts has been in the bank for over an hour, it's now or never. Sebastian opens the car door, steps out and locks the car. He walks briskly across the street and places the letter in the yellow letterbox. His heart pounding he quickly crosses back across the street and unlocks the Bentley. He climbs in and takes a seat. He turns the radio on in an effort to slow his thumping heart and calm his nerves. Sebastian watches the bank's doors. Ten minutes later, Dr. Roberts exits the bank. Sebastian climbs out of the car and stands next to the Bentley. He opens the car door as Dr. Roberts approaches the car. Roberts places his briefcase on the back seat and motions for Sebastian to close the door and lock the car.

"Sebastian, will you join me for a mid-day meal, on me?"

"Yes, sir, I'd be happy to."

Sebastian hasn't been allowed to leave the Chalet much less eat at a sidewalk café in over a year. It almost feels normal except for the hot bulky GPS monitor strapped to his wrist.

"I have concluded my business for the week a few hours early. Would you be so kind as to accompany me to the Louvre this afternoon? Your boss won't be expecting us back at the Chalet until early evening."

"I'd be honored to accompany you, sir." Sebastian can't believe his luck. He has sat in the car for most of the week eating sandwiches out of plastic bags he's been keeping in the glove box and drinking bottled water. Today, he will be eating at a sidewalk café and touring the Louvre.

"Order whatever you like. I'll be claiming it as a business expense." Dr Roberts tells Sebastian.

A beautiful young girl approaches the table and asks for their order. "Have you decided what you'd like to order Sebastian?"

"Yes, I'd like to get a bacon cheeseburger with an order of fries, and a glass of lemonade if that's alright?"

"Sounds great, let's make it two orders exactly the same."

Sebastian puts his menu down and looks at the pretty girl. "Deux hamburgeur avec du bacon et du fromage et une portion de pommes frites avec deux lemonade."

The pretty young server takes their order and walks away. She returns to the table a few moments later with two tall glasses of ice-cold lemonade.

"So, you speak English and French fluently. Where are you from, Sebastian?"

"I grew up in a small orphanage just a few kilometers outside of Paris."

"How did you wind up living and working as an indentured servant at Luscious Corbett's Chalet? Yes, I know you're an indentured servant, are you surprised? I'm aware of the business practices of my dear old friend. I can't say I approve, but his contracts are iron-clad. I'm sorry I can't help you any more than to teach you what it is you need assistance with. Yes, I know about that as well. Luscious has filled me in on your little, shall we say 'problem'." Dr. Roberts explains.

"I was an angry, arrogant child. I had a chip on my shoulder the size of France. I racked up a lot of debt borrowing money and gambling with my future. When I could no longer borrow money the legal way, I found my way to Monsieur Corbett's Chalet. He paid off my debts. When I was unable to pay him back in the allotted time, I was forced into signing one of Monsieur Corbett's iron-clad contracts. I moved into the servant's quarters at the Chalet. My room and board as well as the cost of food and clothing are removed from my wages. The debt never seems to get any smaller. I'm careful what I ask for. Sadly, my recent medical costs means I have no future. My contract I'm afraid is for life." Sebastian sadly explains.

"Do you have any family out there looking for you, anyone at all?" Sebastian waits to answer the question as their food arrives at the table. Sebastian inhales deeply, the smell is intoxicating. Sebastian picks the burger up and takes a large bite. He savors the flavors of smoked bacon and sharp cheddar cheese. He chews slowly, swallows, and takes a long draw of lemonade. He studies Dr. Roberts and tries to decide if he can trust the man before truthfully answering his question.

"There is only Kindle, but she has no idea where to even begin looking for me. I met her in school, her family lives in Paris. As to why she has put up with me all these years I'll never understand. I haven't been an easy person to get along with."

"When was the last time you saw her?"

"A little over a year ago, before I moved to the Chalet. She was preparing for University. We were supposed to start school together in the fall. She will be starting school in the next couple of weeks. I should be joining her at University, instead my arrogance and stupidity landed me in the servitude of Monsieur Corbett. I don't blame anyone. I know it's all on me. I can't change it, so I live it one day at a time."

"Corbett warned me you were brutally honest. I appreciate that. It'll make my job easier."

Sebastian eats his last few bites in silence, finishes his lemonade and waves the young brunette over. Sebastian thanks her for her service and asks for their check in perfect French.

"How many languages do you speak?" Dr. Roberts asks.

"Three. French, English, and a small amount of Italian. The sisters at the orphanage spoke mostly French with a small amount of Italian. I learned English as a second language in school. I also studied Italian on the side. I speak all three fluently now."

"You learned English so you could talk to Kindle, isn't that right?" Dr. Roberts asks.

"Yes sir, how did you know?"

"The look on your face, the sound of your voice when you speak her name. How long will you pine for her?" Dr. Roberts asks as he stands up and prepares to leave.

"Her memory is the only reason I haven't killed myself. The sound of her laughter and the love in her eyes are what keep me going day in and day out. As long as I have her memories the strength to stay alive will endure. Once she's gone, well sir, I don't know." Sebastian mournfully answers as they walk back towards the Bentley. Sebastian unlocks the car, holds the door open, and waits for Dr. Roberts to settle in.

Sebastian starts up the car and pulls out into traffic. "The Louvre, Sir?"

"Yes, please."

"Sebastian, do you have any plans for this evening, say around 8:00, I have tickets to the Opera de la Bastille. Andrew Lloyd Webbers Phantom of the Opera is performing there tonight? I'm sure Luscious will not be rude enough to turn down the personal request of his oldest dearest friend."

"No Sir. I haven't made any plans as of yet. I'll just need to get approval from Monsieur Corbett first."

"Don't you worry about Luscious Corbett, you let me handle him. I know how to get what I want from Luscious."

Sebastian and Dr. Roberts arrive at the Louvre. For the next two hours he enjoys the feeling of being almost human, like a tourist at the Louvre for the first time. Sebastian worries about what Monsieur Corbett will say about his accompanying Dr. Roberts to the Opera House later that night. He decides to leave that request up to Dr.

Roberts and Monsieur Corbett. The afternoon passes all too quickly. Sebastian feels as if they just arrived when it is time to leave and head back to the Chalet.

Traffic is light and the ride back to the Chalet seems to fly by. Sebastian pulls up to the gates and honks the horn twice; the guard waves them in. Sebastian drives the Bentley up to the main guest house. He drops Dr. Roberts at the door and returns the Bentley to the garage. Sebastian fills the tank. He washes and details the car inside and out, returns the remote key to the key box turns and leaves the garage. Sebastian walks back towards the servant's quarters. Francois the ugly gorilla calls him to the main guest house. Francois instructs him to go to Monsieur Corbett's office where Luscious Corbett will be waiting for him. Sebastian enters through the servant's entrance and heads straight for Monsieur Corbett's office. He knocks lightly on the door and waits to be invited in.

"Entrer" Luscious Corbett barks.

Sebastian opens the door and enters the room. Dr. Roberts is standing next to Corbett's desk, Sebastian closes the door and walks to the center of the room. He stands with his hands by his side.

"Sebastian, Dr. Roberts has informed me that he would request your services this evening for a few hours. He has tickets to the Opera de la Bastille and he's in need of your escort services. You are to clean up, change clothes, and report back to the garage to pick up the Bentley in one hour?"

"Oui, Monsieur."

`"Good, you're dismissed." Luscious Corbett impatiently waves him out the door. Sebastian walks calmly out of the building and quickly walks back to the servant's quarters where he shaves and showers. Sebastian changes into that evening's attire. He is to wear a black tuxedo, dress socks and dress shoes. He grabs a small amount of food from the dining hall and heads back to the garage. Sebastian checks out the Bentley's remote key and drives the Bentley up to the main guest house. He parks the car and waits by the rear of the car for Dr. Roberts. Ten minutes later, Dr. Roberts exits the main guest house. Sebastian opens the rear door and assists the kind doctor into the rear of the car. Sebastian enters the Opera de la Bastille into the GPS and follows the instructions into the city to the Opera House. Sebastian pulls up in front of the Opera house, he assists Dr. Roberts out of the vehicle and returns to the driver's seat. He pulls away from the Opera House and finds suitable parking a block from the theatre and parks the car. He gets out and locks the doors. Sebastian considers how easy it would be to lock the car up and just walk away. How far could he make it. How would he remove the GPS device on his wrist? How long before Monsieur Corbett found him and killed him or worse: slowly, painfully tortured him and Sergei in front of the other servants as punishment. He changes his mind and turns towards the opera house. Sebastian quickly walks back to the theatre and joins Dr. Roberts. Sebastian had studied Opera in school but has never been to a live Opera performance. The next few hours pass all too quickly. It is the most magical magnificent evening in Sebastian's life. Something he will not soon forget.

Chapter 6

SEBASTIAN OFFERS TO RETRIEVE THE CAR, BUT DR. ROBERTS insists on walking back to the car with him.

"It's a nice night, let's walk back together. What did you think of the performance?" Dr. Roberts asks Sebastian.

"It was magnificent, I've never experienced anything so beautiful before in my life. Except maybe Kindle. It's not something I'll soon forget."

"Truth time, Sebastian, this is where I come clean with you. I invited you to join me tonight and Luscious Corbett allowed it because I hoped that this evening would inspire you. I mean to say your little problem. This is the part where we talk about it. Do you understand?"

"Yes, Sir."

"I'll explain my meaning as bluntly as possible. The next time you're on your knees or lying in a bed next to a man that you are expected to pleasure, tonight is what I want you to remember. I want you to envision every wonderful thing about tonight's performance in your mind. The mini vacation your bunkmate spoke of. This is where I want you to go. Ignore the pain, ignore the humiliation. Just remember this one magical evening. I can't promise you that it will come easily at first. You will have to find it in yourself to find this place in your memory and have the willpower to pull it out and consume yourself with it. Do you understand, Sebastian?"

"Yes, I have to learn how to remove myself from what's happening and find my place of peace and comfort. My inner strength."

"Correct, Sebastian, do you have that kind of strength in you?"

Sebastian unlocks the car and opens the door for Dr. Roberts. He considers Dr. Roberts' question. "Yes, I can be strong. I promise."

The Bentley pulls up to the Chalets gates. Sebastian honks the horn twice, the gates open. Sebastian drives the Bentley up to the main guest house and assists Dr. Roberts out of the car. "Sebastian, after you have finished checking the car back in, would you be so kind as to join me up in my suite? I'll inform Luscious that you will be joining me instead of returning to your private quarters."

"Yes, Sir."

"Splendid." Dr Roberts responds.

Sebastian climbs back into the Bentley; his stomach ties itself into knots. He knows what he must do, he's just not sure that he can. Sebastian drives back to the garage, wipes the car down with a damp cloth and fills it with gas for tomorrow's trip to the airport. Dr. Roberts will be heading back home in the U.S. tomorrow morning.

Sebastian slowly walks back up to the main guest house. He enters through the side entrance. He stops by Monsieur Corbett's office to inform him that the Bentley is gassed up and ready to leave in the morning. Corbett instructs him that he is to go straight up to Dr. Robert's suite instead of returning to his quarters.

Sebastian slowly walks up the three flights of stairs to Dr. Roberts suit. He knocks on the door and waits. Sebastian enters the room and closes the door behind him. Dr. Roberts pours two glasses of wine and offers one to Sebastian.

"Sebastian, this may make things a little easier. Most men will offer you something to drink. Truth be told most men can't perform without a little liquid courage." Dr. Roberts explains as he hands the glass of wine to Sebastian. Sebastian sips the wine and shifts nervously. "I'm not going to touch you. I'm not going to force myself on you, that's not how this works." Dr. Roberts instructs Sebastian.

Sebastian calms down and takes another sip of wine.

"Would you join me in the bedroom? There are a few less windows and a little more privacy."

Sebastian swallows the last of the wine and sits the glass down, he follows Dr. Roberts into the adjoining room. Dr. Roberts pulls the drapes across the window.

"Do you remember what we spoke of earlier tonight?" Dr. Roberts asks in a soothing calming voice as he takes a seat in a chair across the room.

"Yes sir."

"OK, good, this is the part where you learn to channel your inner strengths. Can you do this for me?"

"Yes." Sebastian's voice wavers. He takes a deep breath and tries to calm his nerves.

"Good, now I need you to remove your clothing and lay them on the foot of the bed."

Sebastian slowly removes his clothing, folds them, and lays them neatly on the foot of the bed. Sebastian stands nude before Dr. Roberts. Every fiber of his being screams at him to cover his nakedness up. But to do so would mean failing Dr. Roberts and in turn failing himself.

"Good, now climb onto the bed and get on your knees in the center of the bed. I promise I'm not going to touch you, that's not what I do. That's not how I operate." Dr. Roberts explains in the exact same calming voice he's been using since Sebastian's arrival in his suit.

Sebastian crawls up onto the king size bed. He gets on his knees and crosses his ankles. He leaves his arms by his side. He can't control the need to cover himself up. To get up and run away as fast as he can. He's promised the doctor that he would be strong, that he would be willing to cooperate. Sebastian has to keep his mind open. Keep his promise.

"Sebastian, I want you to close your eyes and picture the Opera de la Bastille, use your inner strength to ignore your surroundings. Ignore that you are in the middle of a king size bed. Ignore that you are nude and on your knees. Picture your favorite moments from tonight. Can you see it?"

"Yes." Sebastian's voice waivers.

"Would another glass of wine help calm your nerves?"

"Yes, a small amount. I don't want to get drunk."

Dr. Roberts stands up, walks across the room, and picks up the bottle of wine on the nightstand. He pours a small amount of wine into Sebastian's wine glass and cups Sebastian's hands around the glass and steps back.

"Drink this, it'll help. I'll take the glass back when you're finished."

Sebastian sips the wine, savoring its flavor, he holds the glass out. Dr. Roberts takes the wine glass from Sebastian's hand and sits the empty glass on the nightstand next to the bed.

"Feeling better?" Dr. Roberts asks.

"Yes" Sebastian answers more steadily.

"OK, we'll start again, I want you to picture the Opera de la Bastille, I want you to remember and picture your favorite moments from tonight. Use your inner strength to ignore your surroundings and channel your inner strengths. Ignore the fact that you're nude and on your knees, find your calm peaceful place. Can you see it, can you feel it?"

Sebastian reaches deep inside himself; he pictures the opera house all lit up. Envisions the entire evening from beginning to end. His breathing slows down. His body shakes less. Sebastian digs deeper into himself. He remembers the feeling of euphoria as he watched the story unfold. How he had enjoyed the feeling of freedom, an evening out with a friend enjoying box seats at the opera house. His breathing evens out. His body becomes still.

"Sebastian, can you hear me?"

Somewhere off in the distance Sebastian can hear Dr. Roberts' question.

"Yes."

"Good, where are you?"

"The Opera House."

"Good, now tell me, how do you feel?"

"Warm, safe, it almost feels like it's real. Do you know what I mean?" Sebastian whispers in response to the doctor's question.

"Yes, Sebastian I understand. Now listen to my voice, find yourself and explore your own physical body, your manhood. Do you understand?" Dr. Roberts calmly asks.

"Yes." Sebastian gently raises his left hand and caresses his inner thigh. He caresses and strokes the muscle hanging between his legs. He feels it harden and grow as he continues to caress and stroke. His breathing speeds, his hands begin to shake.

"Sebastian, calm down. You're at the opera house. You're alone. No one can see you. You're completely safe. No one can hurt you." Dr. Roberts' voice is soothing. Sebastian calms down. His breathing shallows out, his hands stop shaking. Sebastian becomes calm. His left hand resumes caressing parts of himself he has kept hidden.

"I need you to open your eyes," Dr. Roberts informs Sebastian in a calming voice. Sebastian opens his eyes. Dr. Roberts hands him a hand towel.

"I need you to finish with your eyes open, you're about to climax, you'll need all of your strength to keep your balance on the bed."

Sebastian accepts the towel and wraps it around his penis, he finishes jerking off into the towel. Breathing deeply Sebastian turns red in the face. He closes his eyes and does his best to resist the urge to vomit all over the king size bed.

"It's OK. You are experiencing a natural reaction. No need to feel embarrassed. You're safe. Would you like to go and clean up in private?"

Sebastian shakily climbs off the bed, catches his breath, and forces his legs to hold his weight. Dr. Roberts points him in the direction of the bathroom. Sebastian cleans up before returning to the bedroom. He stands nude at the foot of the bed and awaits further instructions unsure of what comes next.

"Feel better? Would you like to get dressed before we talk about it?" Dr. Roberts asks.

Sebastian quickly gets dressed and sits on the edge of the bed. He takes a few minutes to compose himself. "Is it much different when it's with another person?"

"Honestly, it's going to be a lot different. Until you are comfortable with your own body you will never be comfortable with anyone else's. Do you understand."

"Until I'm no longer ashamed of my own private sexual needs, I will be unable to pleasure another's." Sebastian answers.

"Correct." Dr. Roberts replies.

For the next hour Sebastian and the doctor discuss that night's events. Sebastian begins to feel more comfortable with himself and what he's capable of doing. Sebastian explores and gets to know his body and mind deeper than ever before. He learns to pleasure and comfort his own needs. He leaves the doctor's suit and returns to his quarters a little braver than before. Sebastian is able to sleep peacefully in his bed for the first time in months without the aid of alcohol, painkillers, or peppermint oil.

Chapter 7

SEBASTIAN WIPES THE BENTLEY DOWN ONE LAST TIME BEFORE climbing in and starting up the car. He drives the car to the main guest house and parks at the front doors. He gets out and loads the doctor's luggage into the trunk placing his briefcase on the floor of the car. He closes the door and awaits Monsieur Corbett's and Dr. Robert's arrival.

Ten minutes later, Dr. Roberts and Monsieur Corbett step out the front doors. Sebastian opens the rear door and waits.

"Sebastian, you will drive Dr. Roberts to Charles de Gaulle Airport. You will accompany him to his gate in terminal two. After assisting the good doctor, you will walk three gates to your left and meet an old friend of yours and mine. You will chauffeur him back here to the Chalet. You of course remember our dear friend Hunter Ryan?"

Luscious Corbett studies Sebastian's face. He looks for any sign of weakness, any sign of panic.

"Oui, Monsieur." Sebastian rigidly answers as all the color drains from his face. A frigid cold consumes him.

Dr. Roberts takes notice of Sebastian's discomfort, his frigid response to Hunter Ryan's name. He makes a mental note to address the issue with Sebastian during their ride to the airport.

Sebastian closes the passenger door and opens the driver door and climbs in. He looks towards Monsieur Corbett one last time. Luscious Corbett smirks evilly at Sebastian. Sebastian considers running him over with the car but just as quickly changes his mind.

Sebastian starts the car, backs up and pulls around to the gate. The GPS monitor on his left wrist feels like it weighs ten pounds. For the first time, he can feel it pressing against his wrist. Sebastian honks the horn twice, the gates open. Sebastian pulls out and turns the Bentley in the direction of the airport.

"Sebastian, everything alright this morning?" Dr. Roberts asks after several minutes. Silence engulfs the vehicle.

"Sebastian?"

Sebastian clears his throat. "Yes, sir we should be at the airport in a little over an hour."

"You don't lie to well Sebastian. What about Hunter Ryan scares you? Makes you so nervous?"

Sebastian nervously fidgets, clears his throat a few times before nervously answering. "Hunter Ryan is the reason Monsieur Corbett invited you to come and stay at the Chalet. Hunter Ryan is the reason I was in need of your services." Sebastian weakly answers.

"I see. Sebastian you're a strong man, you will be alright. Just remember the Opera House. You're a smart, strong-willed man. You can overcome your fears. You can do whatever's asked of you."

"I hope you're right sir. I guess we'll find out soon enough." Sebastian weakly answers.

Traffic is light, they arrive at the airport on time. Sebastian carries the doctor's luggage to the Air France counter and checks in the doctor's luggage. He accompanies Dr. Roberts to terminal two. The flight is on time. Sebastian shakes hands with the doctor one last time.

"I'm sorry there isn't more I could do for you. My services at the Chalet are contingent upon my staying impartial to Luscious Corbett's business practices. Promise me you'll remember our sessions. Promise me you'll visit the opera as often as possible."

"Thank you, doctor. I promise I'll remember. I'll be strong." Sebastian answers. Dr. Roberts smiles "I'm holding you to that promise." He turns and walks down the corridor. Sebastian feels a renewed strength coursing through his veins.

Sebastian turns and walks three gates to the left; he learns that Hunter Ryan's flight has been delayed by weather. Sebastian takes a seat and stares at the yellow letterbox across the terminal. He pulls out his pad of paper and a pen. Sebastian addresses the envelope and affixes the correct postage. He writes a quick letter to Kindle, stuffs the letter in the addressed envelope and seals it. Sebastian glances nervously around the terminal before getting up and walking over to the letterbox. Sebastian stuffs the letter into the letterboxes opening. He wonders what would happen if Luscious ever found out about Kindle. If Luscious ever found out about his letters to her. He fears the answer to his own question. He fears for her life as well as her families. Luscious could never know.

My Dearest Kindle,

I have met an amazing doctor who has helped me to find my inner strength; I am stronger than I give myself credit for. I have found my inner peace, my place of solitude. The place where I can feel safest.

I have learned to channel my anger; I release what I can no longer face. I search for the answers that are available to me. I will never know who I am, or where I came from. I can accept that, it's time to move forward. It's time for me to be the man that I am.

Have you started university? Have you moved on campus? I only wish I had a way of tracking your progress. Kindle you're an amazing woman. You're a gifted interior designer, you will succeed in your desires. I only hope that these letters will continue to find you once you're attending University.

Much Love,
Sebastian

Swiss International Airlines announces Hunter Ryan's flight. Like a kick in the gut, Sebastian's stomach aches. He fights the urge to run. Sebastian collects himself and holds up Mr. Ryan's marquee sign. Hunter Ryan arrives with the first-class passengers. Sebastian nervously greets Mr. Ryan and takes his briefcase and carry-on luggage.

"Baggage Claim Monsieur?" Sebastian asks.

"No, I'm traveling light, short trip this time. You look familiar. Have we met before? Yes, of course you're the reluctant offering?" Hunter Ryan answers his own question.

"Oui Monsieur, I'm sorry it won't happen again. Are you ready? I'm parked right out front sir?" Sebastian answers his voice barely audible, unable to look Hunter Ryan in the face.

Sebastian escorts Mr. Ryan to the Bentley and places his bags on the trunk. Sebastian opens the rear door and assists Mr. Ryan into the back of the car. He hands Mr. Ryan his briefcase and shuts the door. He returns to the trunk and loads Mr. Ryan's two small bags in the trunk.

Sebastian climbs into the driver's seat and starts the car. He carefully pulls out into traffic and heads back towards the Chalet. "We should arrive at the Chalet in a little over an hour Mr. Ryan, is there anything you need sir?" Sebastian asks.

"No, thank you." Hunter Ryan studies Sebastian's nervous face reflecting from the car's rear-view mirror. Sebastian turns his gaze towards the road and tries his best to ignore Hunter Ryan's gaze.

Sebastian turns the radio on. Comforting classical music like the kind Monsieur Corbett listens to plays from the car speakers. The drive through the countryside is beautiful, it reminds Sebastian of the drive to Kindle's house. An hour later, Sebastian pulls the Bentley up to the Chalet's gates, honks the horn twice and waits. The gates open. Sebastian drives through the gates and drives around to the main guest house. Sebastian parks the car, gets out and opens Mr. Ryan's door. Sebastian assists Hunter Ryan out of the vehicle. He walks to the rear of the car and pops the trunk; he removes the luggage and follows him through the doors to the front counter. Hunter Ryan checks in. Sebastian follows him to his suite and lays his luggage on the luggage rack.

"Anything else I can do for you, sir?" Sebastian nervously asks.

"No, thank you." Hunter Ryan answers. He studies Sebastian's demeanor as he exits the room.

Sebastian heads back down the stairs and across the foyer.

"Sebastian, after you have washed and detailed the car, return to my office." Corbett calls out to Sebastian as he exits the building.

"Oui, Monsieur." Sebastian's heart pounds in his chest as he walks out the door. He can guess what it is Monsieur Corbett wishes to speak with him about.

Sebastian drives the Bentley to the garage, parks the car and turns the remote key in. He fills the Bentley up with gas, washes, details, vacuums, and deodorizes the interior. An hour and a half later, he heads back up to Monsieur Corbett's office, his stomach doing flip flops in his gut. Sebastian enters through the servant's entrance. He walks to Corbett's office and knocks on the door. "Entrez." Corbett instructs.

Sebastian opens the door, enters the room, and closes the door. Sebastian turns and walks to the center of the room and stands with his arms by his side. Corbett looks up and opens his top desk drawer. The leather strap is now accompanied by a thick wooden paddle with holes drilled in it. Corbett walks around to the front of his desk, ignoring the open drawer. "Sebastian, Hunter Ryan has requested you as his personal offering this evening. You won't have a problem with this request, will you?"

"Non, Monsieur." Sebastian answers as he nervously eyes the open desk drawer. He can only imagine the pain caused by a thick wooden paddle with holes drilled in it. "2030, Sebastian. Oh, and Sebastian don't make him wait." Corbett walks back around his desk and closes the top desk drawer. Corbett takes a seat in his leather chair and stares at Sebastian. Sebastian lowers his eyes to the floor.

"You may leave. 2030, Sebastian, don't disappoint me." Corbett stands and walks to his mini bar as Sebastian turns to leave. "Oui Monsieur." Sebastian weakly answers as he walks out the door. Sebastian returns to his quarters, undresses, and steps into the shower. Sebastian groans as he vomits all over the shower stall, His stomach flip flops as he tries to regain his composure. Sergei returns and hears the shower running. He opens the bathroom door and peeks in. "Everything, alright, man? We've been instructed to report to the stables." Sebastian turns the shower off, wraps a towel around his midsection and steps out. "I'll dress and be right behind you, man."

"I'll wait. We'll walk down together." Sergei steps out of the bathroom and gives Sebastian privacy to dress. Sebastian brushes his teeth, combs his hair and dresses in jeans and a short-sleeved shirt. He steps out looking like a handsome eighteen-year-old boy. Sebastian and Sergei head out of the servant's quarters and walk down to the stables. They step through the doors and stop dead in their tracks. Hanging from the rafters is the badly beaten and abused body of Jade. A beautiful young female servant from Hong Kong. Sebastian had gotten to know her pretty well over the last year and a half that she'd been working at the Chalet. Jade worked both in housekeeping and as a private offering to the wealthier clients in the evening hours. She was only 20 years old. Jade was dead and there was nothing they could do to return life to her limp hanging lifeless body. Luc shoves two shovels into Sebastian's hands and instructs Sergei to climb up and lower Jades body down from the rafters. Luc instructs them to wrap her body in the white cloth lying on the ground. They are to dig a grave six feet deep and bury her. Luc leaves the stables and returns to the main guest house.

Sergei climbs up into the rafters and pulls at the ropes, able to loosen them enough he slowly lowers her body down to Sebastian's waiting arms. Sebastian cradles Jade's body against his chest. He wants to scream and cry. Sergei climbs down from the rafters and assists Sebastian with wrapping Jade's body in the thin white bed cloth. Sebastian carries her body into the tree line of the woods, he lays her body down and begins digging.

"What happened? Who did this?" Sebastian angrily asks.

"Rumor is Francois lost his temper; you notice he wasn't with Luc. I worked in the kitchens of the main guest house earlier today. I overheard Francois and Jade arguing. Luc came and told me that Monsieur Corbett wanted to speak with me. I was to meet him in the parlor instead of his office. When I walked by Monsieur Corbett's office on my way to the parlor, I saw Francois standing in the center of Corbett's office with his shirt removed. Francois had angry red welts across his back. Like the ones I had after my beating. Francois's hands were flex cuffed. His ankles were restrained by leather straps attached to two wooden boards on the floor. I guess so he couldn't run. I entered the parlor and Monsieur Corbett was waiting for me. Corbett told me that you had just returned from the airport. He told me that there had been an incident in the stables. I was to tell you to meet me in the stables and to follow Luc's instructions. We are not to tell anyone what has happened. We're to keep silent." Sergei rolls his eyes angrily towards the Chalet.

"He raped her and beat her? Did he also hang her?" Sebastian asks.

"I think he hung her; those ropes were tight. There are marks on the beams up there where the rope cut into the wood as he pulled her body into the air. After a beating like that I doubt she would have had the strength to hang herself." Sergei answers.

Sergei and Sebastian put their shovels down and walk over to Jade's body. Sebastian cradles her wrapped body against his chest and gently lifts her body up off the cold ground. He gently places her body in the damp cold earth. He walks out to the field and grabs two handfuls of wildflowers, he places one handful on top of her body and lays the second bundle of flowers off to the side. Sergei and Sebastian cover her body with the loose dirt. When they're finished, Sebastian lays his shovel down and recites Dylan Thomas' Poem, Do not go gentle into that good night. When Sebastian is finished Sergei lays the second bunch of wildflowers on Jade's grave. They return to the stables in silence. They silently clean up any evidence left by Jade's death and their efforts to care for her broken body.

Sergei and Sebastian both skip dinner, they return quietly to their room both lost in their own deep thoughts. Saddened and angered by Jade's senseless death. Sebastian undresses and showers for the second time that day. Sebastian dresses in his black silk robe. He stares at his reflection in the mirror and prays for the first time in over a year to a God he no longer believes in for the strength he'll need to make it through the night.

Chapter 8

Dressed in his black silk offering robes as requested by Monsieur Corbett, Sebastian knocks on Hunter Ryan's door at exactly 2030. "Entrer." Hunter Ryan softly answers. Sebastian enters the room and closes the door behind him. He walks to the center of the room and faces Hunter Ryan. Sebastian takes a deep breath. With his heart pounding, ice daggers forming in his chest, and voice shaking Sebastian addresses Mr. Ryan. "How may I help you?" Hunter Ryan walks around Sebastian, pours two drinks and offers one to Sebastian. Without hesitation Sebastian accepts the glass of red wine and swallows the entire glass in one gulp. The red wine spreads through his body like wildfire giving him the liquid courage he needs to stand still and not run. "You scared? Your first time?" Hunter Ryan asks.

"Oui Monsieur." Why lie? It will be apparent enough.

"Would a second drink calm your nerves?" Hunter Ryan asks.

"Oui, Monsieur." Sebastian nervously answers.

Hunter Ryan pours a second glass of red wine and hands it to Sebastian, "Sip it. Don't gulp, it'll go straight to your head. You'll be no use to me passed out drunk."

Sebastian accepts the second glass of wine and slowly sips it. Hunter Ryan walks behind Sebastian and unhooks Sebastian's robes. The black silk material falls to the floor. Sebastian inhales deeply the scent of peppermint oil rubbed into his arms and hands. The scent soothes him. Sebastian steps away from his robes on the floor. He is left standing in a pair of matching black briefs. Sebastian sits the glass of wine down on the closest table. Hunter Ryan places his hand on Sebastian's back and guides him towards the bedroom. Sebastian follows. He digs deep into his memories and searches for the place that houses the Opera de la Bastille. He drops to his knees, crosses his ankles, closes his eyes, and opens his mouth. Hunter Ryan stands in front of him and lowers his pants. Sebastian leans in towards Mr. Ryan and goes to the opera. Two hours later Sebastian exits the suite and returns to his quarters. Sebastian disrobes and removes his briefs. He climbs into the shower and turns it on as hot as he can handle it. Sebastian's body shakes as he vomits and cries like a child. Sebastian scrubs his body till it is red, raw, and sore. The shower turns cold. Sebastian climbs out and just sits on the floor. Sick, he crawls to the toilet. It has got to get easier. The humiliation and pain will lessen over time the doctor had told him. The first time would be the hardest, that's what the doctor had said.

Sergei finds Sebastian's nude and shivering body curled up in the fetal position on the cold bathroom tile floor an hour and a half later. Sergei sits on the floor next to Sebastian. He pulls Sebastian into the seated position and wraps a towel around his cold naked shivering body. He rubs his hands up and down Sebastian's arms. He rubs his back and tries to comfort him. After ten minutes Sergei goes out to the main room and gets Sebastian a clean pair of briefs and a pair of sweatpants. Sergei returns to the bathroom, and pulls Sebastian to his feet and hands him the clothing. "Come out when you're ready."

Sebastian pulls the clean clothing on, runs a brush through his hair and brushes his teeth for the fifth time that night. He walks out and sits on his bed. Sebastian stares at the floor.

"Are you going to be OK? Did he hurt you?" Sergei asks with the care and concern of a brother trying to protect his own.

"I'm OK. He didn't abuse me if that's what you're asking. Actually, compared to the stories I've heard, he was rather patient and gentle." Sebastian shakily whispers.

"Good, sometimes they can be rough or abusive." Sergei drapes a cotton blanket around Sebastian's shivering body. "You sure you're alright? You look pretty shaken up."

"Just cold, I'll be alright." Sebastian lays his head down on his thin pillow, closes his eyes and tries to sleep.

Sergei shuts the lights off and pushes his bed next to Sebastian's. Sergei lies down next to Sebastian's shivering body. "Just till you stop shaking. I promise."

Sebastian mumbles thanks and quietly falls into an uneasy sleep. Sergei waits till he knows that Sebastian is asleep and warm enough before quietly pushing his bed back to the other side of the room. Sergei climbs into bed, covers himself and watches Sebastian's restless sleep a few more minutes before allowing sleep to overtake him.

Sebastian wakes first. Sergei's bed is back on his side of the room. True to his word he hadn't pushed Sebastian.

"Merci, you're a good friend." Sebastian thanks Sergei over morning croissants.

"You'd have done the same for me."

Sergei and Sebastian spend the day in the kitchens washing dishes, scrubbing baseboards, mopping the floors, and shining every piece of stainless steel in the kitchen.

At 1830, dressed in a jade green robe, Sebastian knocks on Hunter Ryan's door. Upon being told to enter, Sebastian opens the door, steps in, closing the door behind him. Sebastian removes his robe and drops to his knees. Hunter Ryan reaches out and pulls Sebastian to his feet. "Not tonight. Put your robes back on. I have other plans. Would you join me out on the veranda?"

Sebastian pulls his robes back on. Confused, he walks out onto the veranda behind Hunter Ryan. There is a small table with two chairs. There is a bottle of white wine and a cheese and cracker tray. Hunter

Ryan invites Sebastian to take a seat. He offers him a glass of white wine. "Does anyone ever just want to talk?" Hunter Ryan asks.

"No, Monsieur, most of the clientele isn't interested in paying for conversation. An offering is the same price regardless of what the offering is used for."

"Blunt and truthful. That can be dangerous." Hunter Ryan comments.

"I'm sorry, Monsieur. Was that offensive?"

"No. I asked, you answered truthfully. I wouldn't ask any less of you." Hunter Ryan shakes his head and laughs.

"How long have you served Luscious Corbett's best interests?" Hunter Ryan asks.

"Almost a year and a half, Monsieur."

"Why do you serve? Why don't you just leave? You're smart, you don't belong here. Any fool can see that." Hunter Ryan asks Sebastian as he pours two glasses of wine.

"Until my debts are paid. I'm under contract."

"I'm sorry to hear that. You have no way out?"

"Non, Monsieur."

"Sebastian, the offerings here, they fear me. Why?"

"Honestly?"

"Isn't that what I'm paying for? Yes, I would expect nothing less from you than the cold honest truth. Remember?"

"I'm sorry, Monsieur Ryan, it is said that you are aggressive towards the Chalet's offerings."

"Is that why you ran the first time?" Hunter. Ryan asks.

"Non, Monsieur"

"Before last night, you hadn't been with a man before."

"That apparent?" Sebastian asks embarrassedly.

"I can just tell. Last night, you went someplace else?"

"Oui, I have a safe haven. I'm sorry if you weren't pleased last night. I can do better if you'll allow me a second chance." Sebastian nervously answers.

"That's unnecessary, as you say, I can be a bit aggressive. I knew you were nervous last night. I knew that being with another man was new to you. I thought maybe I had hurt you the way you rushed out after I dismissed you last night." Hunter Ryan makes eye contact with Sebastian.

"Embarrassed, yes. Injured, no."

"It'll get easier with time. I promise it won't always be so rough." Hunter Ryan informs Sebastian.

"That's what I've been told. I hope it's true, Monsieur Ryan."

"Sebastian, you said that you owe a debt, that you are under a contract. But what keeps you here? What keeps you from running?" Hunter Ryan asks.

"We're not allowed to leave the Chalet without permission, or without a GPS wrist monitor."

"What would happen if you tried to leave tonight without permission and without one of those monitors?"

"Monsieur Corbett would release the dogs. I would be hunted down, shot on site for breach of contract. Desertion. Or worse publicly beaten and tortured as a reminder to fellow servants what happens to those who breach their contracts." Sebastian nervously answers.

"I'm sorry I asked. You don't belong here. I hope you find a way to pay off your debts."

"I have an early flight tomorrow morning and your boss Monsieur Corbett tells me you will be my chauffeur. I dismiss you for the night. Thank you for your brutal honesty and conversation. Sometimes it's just nice to get to know the person. Goodnight Sebastian."

"Goodnight Monsieur Ryan." Sebastian leaves the suite and heads back to his small room in the servant's quarters.

Francois, stripped nude, whipped and beaten, hands flex cuffed behind his back walks down the cold dark hallway of the servant's quarters. Most have gone to bed, but a few like Sebastian and Sergei returning from late night rendezvous are present to watch Francois' walk of shame. No longer protected by his rich uncle he is forced to live amongst those whose lives he has made a living hell day in and day out. They are the ones Francois fears most.

Jurai, Francois' replacement for second in command, shoves Francois toward the smallest room at the end of the hallway. The room next to the common area and across the hall from the open shower room. The room for those who hadn't earned private rooms with their own showers. There is no door, only a dark colored piece of fabric covering the entrance. Francois steps into his new room. There is no window, no furniture except for a small twin-size mattress on the floor. No blankets, no pillow, just a fitted sheet and a top sheet to cover up with. The rest of the bedding he would have to earn like everyone else. Next to the mattress is an empty wooden box. Francois will be allowed to use this for his seven days-worth of clothing, toothbrush, toothpaste, comb, bar of soap, wash rag, thin towel and a small bottle of shampoo.

A GPS monitor is fastened to Francois' left wrist and his flex cuffs are cut off. Francois is left alone, cold and shivering in his small room with no door. Francois turns the light switch on and dresses quickly. He places the other six outfits in the wooden box, picks up the fitted sheet and stretches it across the twin-size mattress. He sits on the mattress, his back against the wall. His eyes on the curtain covering the entrance to his room. He wraps the second sheet around his body and waits. He knows what is coming. He saw the looks of revenge on their eager young faces as he was paraded down the hallway. You don't kill the help! It was a lesson Francois' uncle planned on teaching him the hard way.

Francois had come to live at his uncle's Chalet when he was 13. Francois' parents had died in a plane crash, and his uncle had been his only living relative. Corbett's son Luc had been 15. Luc and Francois became inseparable. Corbett nicknamed them trouble one and younger trouble two. When they came of age, they both were guaranteed jobs at the Chalet. They both had a mean streak in them so there had been no trouble placing them in charge of the indentured servants contracted to work at the Chalet.

It took less than 15 minutes for the gang of six men to assemble. Francois never stood a chance.

Chapter 9

SEBASTIAN WAKES UP EARLY. QUIETLY SO AS NOT TO WAKE Sergei he showers and dresses in his chauffeur clothing. Sebastian reports to Monsieur Corbett's office to have the GPS monitor fitted to his left wrist. He walks down to the garage and checks out the remote key to the Bentley. He drives up to the main guest house. He parks the Bentley and walks up to Mr. Ryan's suit. Sebastian knocks on the door.

"Good morning, Monsieur Ryan, May I take your luggage down to the car?" Sebastian asks.

"Yes, that would be fine."

Sebastian picks up the two small duffel bags and reaches for Hunter Ryan's briefcase. "Sebastian, leave the briefcase, I'll bring it down when I check out."

Sebastian turns and leaves the suit carrying the two small duffel bags. Sebastian loads the two small bags into the trunk, as he shuts the trunk, he watches Dr. Maboob's vehicle pull onto the grounds. The doctor drives straight towards the servant's quarters. Sebastian has a pretty good idea why the doctor has been called this early in the morning. Sebastian had heard part of the scuffle last night and was still awake when Sergei had returned to their room 30 minutes later. Sergei had headed straight for the shower even though he had showered earlier in the evening.

Hunter Ryan walks out of the main guest house. Sebastian opens the car door and assists Mr. Ryan into the car.

"Sebastian we will be stopping by my bank in Paris before heading to the airport this morning." Hunter Ryan informs Sebastian.

"No problem, is Monsieur Corbett aware of the change in plans?"

"Yes."

Sebastian closes the door. He climbs in, buckles up and types the bank's name and address into the GPS as Hunter Ryan recites it aloud. Sebastian starts the car, drives to the gates, and honks the horn twice. The gates open; Sebastian pulls out into traffic and heads towards Paris.

Sebastian pulls up to Banque De France. Hunter Ryan instructs Sebastian to stay with the car and await his return. Sebastian gets back into the Bentley and turns on the radio. He listens to the morning weather and traffic report. Sebastian waits 20 minutes before Hunter Ryan returns with a larger briefcase than the one he entered the bank with. Sebastian opens the passenger door for Mr. Ryan and holds the newer heavier briefcase while Hunter Ryan climbs into the Bentley. Sebastian sets the briefcase on the floor of the car next to Mr. Ryan's feet and closes the door.

Sebastian starts the car and pulls out into traffic. "Charles De Gaulle airport Monsieur Ryan?" Sebastian asks.

"No we'll be returning to the Chalet. I have a meeting with Luscious Corbett upon our return."

Confused Sebastian turns the car around and heads back towards the Chalet. Sebastian pulls up to the gates, honks the horn twice and waits. The gates open, he drives the car around to the main guest house. "Sebastian you look confused?"

"Oui, Monsieur."

"Sebastian I'm a contract purchaser. Luscious supplies me with young ladies for my business in Chex Le Bart, Switzerland. I'll be honest I've looked into purchasing your contract. I could use a personal assistant of your caliber. Unfortunately, Luscious Corbett has no interest in selling your contract for any amount of Euros at this time." Hunter Ryan confesses.

"Stay with the car, my business with Luscious shouldn't take long." Hunter Ryan instructs Sebastian as he exits the vehicle. Mr. Ryan saunters up the front walk and enters the Main Guest House. Sebastian turns his attention towards the stables. Francois is limping towards the horse's stables. Beaten black and blue Sebastian is amazed he lived through last night's beating. He feels no pity for the murderer, only anger that he lives while Jade lies six feet deep in the cold damp ground. Sebastian wonders whose contracts Hunter Ryan is purchasing. Sebastian associates with the female servant's very little. The sexes are kept apart from one another except when being offered up as personal offerings together. Some preferred both sexes while others are a little more particular as to their sexual preference. Sebastian wonders if he will recognize the merchandise or if he'll even know them. When had lives turned so easily into merchandise in his mind. It sickened and angered him that he had even referred to innocent lives in such a manner.

Hunter Ryan exits the main guest house with two young Asian girls in their early teens. He has never seen these girls before. Sebastian is sickened by the realization that he finds relief in not recognizing the two young girls. Sickened by the fact that it makes it easier for him to look them in the face as he watches them being escorted by Mr. Ryan back towards the car. Sebastian steps out of the car and opens the rear passenger door. The girls are pushed in first followed by Hunter Ryan with a now empty briefcase in his hand. The trip to the bank this morning had been to make a rather large withdrawal to cover the payment of the two young girls' contracts. Sebastian starts the car and pulls up to the gates, honks the horn twice and waits. The gates open he pulls away from the Chalet and heads back towards Paris.

"Charles De Gaulle airport, Monsieur?"

Hunter Ryan nods.

Sebastian keeps his eyes on the road; he cannot bring himself to look at the two young Asian girls in the back of the car. They're eyes pleading for Sebastian's help. There is nothing he can do to help them. Sebastian hates himself. He wants to wreck the car but with his luck he would live long enough to be tortured and shot upon his return to Monsieur Corbett's Chalet. Sebastian knows he is a coward; he wishes he were stronger. He wishes he had the gall to pull the car over and drag Hunter Ryan out of the back of the car. To beat him until his arms were too heavy to land another blow. Sebastian would then drive the girls to safety. Where could he drive them that Monsieur Corbett wouldn't be able to find them.

The rain causes delays but not enough for Hunter Ryan to miss his flight. Sebastian pulls up to the airport and removes their luggage from the trunk. Hunter Ryan instructs each girl to take a bag. Mr. Ryan carries the now empty briefcase and three passports. Sebastian watches as the two young girls walk terrified hand in hand towards the airport terminal. He prays to a God he no longer believes in that he will not see Monsieur Ryan ever again. He isn't sure if he was supposed to be thankful that Hunter Ryan had tried to purchase his contract or just disgusted. Sebastian pulls away from the airport and back out into traffic. He points the Bentley in the direction of the Chalet. The rain lets up and the sun comes out. Sebastian arrives back at the Chalet in a little over an hour. Sebastian drives straight to the garage, washes, and details the car, fills it with gas and turns the remote key in. Sebastian reports to Monsieur Corbett that he is back and that he has washed and detailed the car. Sebastian asks no questions about Hunter Ryan's business or about the two young Asian girls. It is none of his business.

Sebastian exits the office and heads back towards the servant's quarters. Sebastian enters the small room he shares with Sergei. Sergei is changing clothes after working in the kitchen all morning. He is changing into his everyday work clothing. A surge of anger flashes through him. He stares at Sergei and releases his anger, his frustration, all his rage towards Sergei.

"Did it feel good? Were you punished for beating him?" Sebastian angrily shouts at Sergei.

"Yeah, it felt great. He deserved it. He raped and killed Jade. And why? Because she wouldn't love him back. His uncle no longer protects him. No one cares about him now. No, I wasn't punished." Sergei yells back.

"Are you finished? Will you attack him again?" Sebastian angrily asks.

"Why do you care? Don't you want to punch him? He's the reason you were beaten so brutally, the reason Dr. Maboob had to be called to save your life." Sergei angrily shouts.

"No! You're wrong. I don't care about that murderer. I would love to punch his lights out. But what would that accomplish? It wouldn't take away the scars he left. I just wondered when you would let go of the anger and move on." Sebastian bitterly asks.

"It was a one-time thing. I've already moved on. Once was enough. I'm not looking to be publicly punished, publicly humiliated. I just needed a little payback for that whipping I was forced to take a few weeks ago." Sergei angrily answers.

"Is that the kind of men we are?" Sebastian bitterly asks.

"I told you it was a one-time deal. It's over. Let it go man." Sergei urges him.

"Alright, I'll drop it. I'm to report to grass cutting detail, how about you?" Sebastian asks.

"Landscaping detail around the main guest house. See you later." Sergei dashes out the door before Sebastian can go on the rampage again.

Sebastian changes his clothes and heads towards the lawn shed to check out his mower for the afternoon. He gets lucky and is given one of the new turn 360 mowers. Hot work but it's better than walking and pushing a mower all day in the baking hot sun. Sebastian hates to admit it, but it felt good to release some of his anger and frustration out on Sergei. He will apologize to him later. For now, he enjoys the feeling of having let off a little steam.

Chapter 10

WHEN A NEWBORN INFANT CHILD IS ABANDONED AT THE hospital, the nurse on duty calls the police. The prints, photographs, and personal information on the child, their name, if known, age, sex, and birth marks are entered into the Euro-national Police Database before the child is taken to a local orphanage. The orphanage updates the child's photograph and information once a year until the child is either adopted, transferred, or leaves the orphanage of their own free will. When a child runs away or is determined missing the orphanage checks in with the police locale, hospitals, and morgues for thirty days and then closes the child's file. The files are delivered to the police locale twice a year where most eventually wind up filed away with the cold case files never to see the light of day again.

Inspector Christian Raines loves his job. Raines served as an officier de police for eight years before being promoted to inspector. Raines has a beautiful wife named Jenna and a lovely daughter named Kindle. He loves both with all his heart. Christian would do anything for his family to keep them safe. At the age of sixteen Christian Raines' daughter had wanted nothing more than to study interior design in New York City in the United States. Kindle was head over heels in love with a young boy from the local orphanage who wanted nothing more than to study architecture. The two dreamt of building and designing homes and offices all over Paris. When the young boy disappeared a year and a half ago at the age of sixteen, Inspector Raines feared the worst.

Christian Raines had filed and easily won power of attorney over the orphan's case file. Five days after Sebastian's disappearance, he had helped his daughter file a missing person's report with the Worldwide National Database for Missing and Exploited Children. In the beginning, Inspector Raines had investigated the boy's disappearance on a daily basis. Hourly updates and missing posters were put up everywhere. Inspector Raines found out that like most orphans, the young man didn't have a lot of money. The boy was massively in debt at the time of his disappearance. He had borrowed money legally at first but when unable to pay the money back, he had turned to darker means to pay back his loans. He began street fighting and stripping at local clubs on the weekends. He had tried to earn enough to pay off his debts. The night of his disappearance, he had been the last one to check out of the strip club. No one saw which direction he had taken upon leaving the strip club that final night. That's where all leads stopped and all evidence turned ice cold.

A year and a half later, the young man's file remained in Inspector Raines' bottom desk drawer. Once a month he pulled the file out and made some phone calls, emailed the boy's photo and information to the local precincts, hospitals, and morgues. With no hits the file would be returned to his bottom desk drawer until the next month's inquiries.

Inspector Raines' daughter Kindle never gave up hope. Once a week, she knocked on her father's office door and inquired into the investigation of her missing fiancé. Slowly over time, Kindle mourned his disappearance. Headstrong, she continued with her studies. Kindle graduated and was accepted to New York University. Kindle was leaving for New York in a few weeks planning to study Interior Design at NYU. Inspector Raines learned from his wife, Jenna, that every few weeks his daughter would receive a letter. These letters were always the same. Plain white envelope, no return post. The envelopes were cheap and could be bought anywhere in the country. Sometimes the letters were postmarked from Paris other times Belgium. It always had the same masculine handwriting on the envelope. Jenna Raines was certain the letters had something to do with Kindle's missing fiancé, she wanted to ask her daughter about the letters but didn't want to invade Kindle's privacy. Jenna Raines photographed the envelopes with the camera on her cell phone before giving the letters to Kindle. Jenna would give the photographs of the envelopes to Christian. Kindle read the letters and hid them from her parents. Christian suspected that the letters were from her missing fiancé as well. Certain that he was still alive but unable to tell his daughter where he was Christian Raines feared the worst for the still living missing young man.

Inspector Raines kept the young man's file at his desk and continued to make inquiries into his disappearance. Inspector Raines checked hospitals, morgues, and precincts in Belgium, Paris, all over France and England. Inspector Raines wouldn't give up. Kindle deserved answers. Answers only Christian could get, answers he would get one way or another.

Chapter 11

Sebastian showers and changes into his dark plum offering robes. If tonight's unannounced visit to Monsieur Corbett's office results in his being punished it would be easiest for him to remove his robes quickly. It has been a month, and someone needs to speak up. Francois will not last much longer. He is pale with dark circles under his eyes. He has lost so much weight that his clothing hangs off his body like a second skin. Sebastian no longer has the energy or the will to dig another grave, much less a grave for the likes of Francois.

Sebastian passes the dining hall stops and glances in. Francois is eating a small amount of food just inside the door. He swallows without chewing, drinks his small glass of water and returns his plate and glass to the dish washing area. Francois quickly leaves the dining hall brushing past Sebastian without looking up as he walks back to his small living quarters. Sebastian shakes his head, skips dinner and heads straight for Monsieur Corbett's office.

Sebastian can hear Luc and Corbett's voices just on the other side of the door. Sebastian takes a deep breath to steady his nerves and knocks softly on the door. Sebastian patiently waits for his knock to be answered. "Entrez," Luc answers. Sebastian opens the door and enters the room. Sebastian notices the look of confusion on Luc and Monsieur

Corbett's faces as he enters the room. Sebastian closes the door and walks to the center of the room. Sebastian stands stiffly at attention with his arms by his side.

"Sebastian? I'm confused? I don't remember sending for you?" Luscious Corbett questions Sebastian.

"Non, Monsieur."

Luc stares at Sebastian and tries to remember if Sebastian is on the short list of offerings for tonight's entertainment. "Sebastian, I don't recall your name being on the list of offerings this evening?" Luc asks as he looks over the short list of private offering requests sitting on Corbett's desk.

"Non, Monsieur."

Luc and Corbett stare at Sebastian. Sebastian swallows the dry boulder size lump in his throat. Shakily he takes a deep breath and speaks up. "Messieurs permission to speak freely with the knowledge that I accept any punishment that may follow this conversation?"

Corbett amusedly looks at Luc. "This should be interesting."

"I agree. I think you should allow him to speak" Luc amusedly answers. They both take a seat and stare at Sebastian. "Permission granted." Corbett answers.

Sebastian takes a deep breath, swallows another boulder size lump in his throat and begins. "Messieurs, in fear of speaking out of turn, I must speak with you concerning Francois' health and well-being. It's been a month. He eats little and sleeps even less. In his first three weeks, he was beaten, bullied, and raped almost nightly. The only reason they haven't killed him yet is in fear of your retribution. Things have quieted down this week only because of his new regiment. He gets up at 0400 before everyone else and showers in the public shower room. He dresses and takes a small box of cereal and a small bottle of milk out to the stables. He eats his breakfast alone hidden somewhere out in the stables. He stays in the stables until it is time to line up for the daily work details. Lately he has been working with Sergei and I in the fields. They won't attack him during work hours. Instead, they wait for the cover of night. After work he returns to the stables and bathes by means of a water hose and bucket. He feeds and waters the horses before returning to the servant's quarters for dinner. He puts a small amount of food on his plate and swallows without chewing first as fast as he can. Once finished he returns his dishes to the dish washing area and quickly quietly leaves.

Most evenings, he hides till lights out. There are dark circles under his eyes, he is pale and sickly. His cough is getting worse. I have seen him spit up blood on several occasions while working next to him in the fields. He tries to cover how sick he's become. His clothing hangs off his body like a second skin. His ribs poke through his skin and he isn't getting nearly enough to eat or drink, not even close to enough to keep him alive much longer."

Sebastian takes a deep breath and calms his nerves before continuing.

"Messieurs, regarding his living quarters; at the end of my first week, I received a cotton blanket and pillow. The end of my second week a door to my room. By the end of my third week a lock for said door, and by the end of my fourth week I received a box spring and bed frame to go with my mattress. I was also given a small nightstand and lamp. I only bring these items up because Francois has received none of these items. Winter is coming and he won't make it another month, much less another week with such a thin mattress on the floor and only a sheet to wrap himself in." Sebastian takes a deep breath, stares at Monsieur Corbett and awaits his punishment.

"Why do you care so much about the man who murdered one of your own? The man you were forced to clean up after? Yes, I know it was you and your roommate who lowered her body down from the rafters, wrapped her body in a white sheet, dug her grave and buried her body. You even placed wildflowers on her grave. The man that punished you so brutally you ended up at a medical clinic fighting for your life. Why would you stand up for him now?" Luscious Corbett asks.

Sebastian thinks about this. Why does he care so much? Would anyone stand up for him if the tables were turned? That was his answer. "Monsieurs, he is human like me. I would hope that if I were being treated in such a manner, someone would have the strength to stand up for me." Sebastian lowers himself to his knees, crosses his ankles and unhooks his robes allowing the silk material to fall to the floor. Sebastian lowers his head and awaits his punishment. Luc stands and walks across the office. He exits through the door directly behind Sebastian. Sebastian flinches at the sound of a door opening and closing behind him. He assumes that Luc has left the room to retrieve some sort of whip or paddle that will be used to punish him. Sebastian waits. Corbett picks up the phone and orders a door to be delivered to the servant's quarters. Ten minutes pass. Sebastian remains on his knees staring at the floor. The office door opens and closes behind him. Luc reappears, walks up to Sebastian's side, and stands over him.

"Sebastian, stand up. Put your robes back on. I understand why you choose to wear them this evening." Corbett instructs Sebastian.

Sebastian stands up and pulls his robes back up around himself. He fastens the hook at the base of his neck. He raises his eyes from the floor and looks to Corbett for further instructions.

"Raise your arms straight out in front of you. Palms up." Corbett instructs.

Sebastian raises his arms palms up and stretches them straight out in front of him. He awaits the first blow. He stares at the wall behind Corbett's desk. Instead of the strike of a switch or ruler against his arms and hands the soft fabric of cotton is placed in his hands. Sebastian stares at the blanket. Luc places a cotton blanket, small pillow, and a door lock in his outstretched arms. Sebastian looks at Luc. Luc nods and walks back around Corbett's desk. Sebastian cannot believe his luck. He thought for sure he would be whipped or beaten for speaking out. "Merci Messieurs." Sebastian thanks his masters. "It comes with a heavy price, Sebastian. You are now the new hall monitor. If there are any problems, you are my eyes and my ears. Do you understand?" Corbett asks.

"Oui, Monsieur."

"You're dismissed. You may return to the servant's quarters." Luc informs Sebastian.

Sebastian turns to leave the office. He struggles with the door but gets it opened and closed without dropping the blanket, pillow, or door lock. Sebastian walks back to the servant's quarters. Sergei greets him at the entrance and holds the door open for him. He is dressed in matching silk robes. Sergei is heading to the main guest house as part of tonight's entertainment. Sebastian thanks him for his help and watches as Sergei walks barefoot across the cold frozen ground. His own feet aching and cold he turns and heads towards Francois room. Sebastian walks to the end of the hallway and knocks on the newly hung door. "Enterer." Francois nervously answers.

Sebastian pushes his foot against the newly hung door, and it swings open. Francois is standing with his back against the far wall. He stares at Sebastian. Sebastian bends down and places the blanket, pillow, and door lock on his thin mattress. He wonders how much longer till he will be given a box spring and bed frame.

"These are for you. I'll get you some tools to install the lock on the door." Sebastian explains before turning to leave the room. "Merci," Francois chokes out like a bad taste in his mouth. "Vous êtes les bienvenus." Sebastian answers. "I'll be right back." Sebastian tells him as he leaves the room. He thinks about how hard it must have been for Francois to have to thank Sebastian for his help. Sebastian walks down the hallway to his small room. He retrieves a small tool kit from his nightstand and a pack of peanut butter crackers. He returns to Francois' room. Francois is tucking his new cotton blanket around his thin mattress. Sebastian helps Francois attach the lock to his door. "You'll be safe now. Here eat this, you need them more than I. You look ghostly thin." Sebastian hands Francois the small pack of crackers he'd been saving to eat later since he had missed dinner. "Merci." Francois answers. Sebastian packs up his tool kit and turns to leave. Francois clears his throat. Sebastian turns to face him. "You never came for me. Why? I thought of everyone you would be the first one out for revenge. I waited night after night. It's your revenge I fear the most." Sebastian thinks about this. "One cannot live in the past. Why is it you think I seek personal revenge?"

"You two were best friends. She loved you, not me. I punished you. Sent you to the Medical Clinic at death's door."

Sebastian thinks long and hard before speaking. "That's why you killed her? Because she didn't love you. Was the baby yours? If your uncle found out about the baby he would have killed both of you. You were trying to save your own thick skin? Guess that plan had a sick twist in the end." Sebastian angrily answers. "And yes, we were close friends. Sort of, so to speak. We never slept together. When I buried her body, she had a baby bump. You killed her and murdered your own son or daughter. Your own flesh and blood." Sebastian angrily answers. Sebastian turns to leave the room again.

"You told no one?" Francois nervously asks.

"It wouldn't bring her or her unborn child back. No, I told no one. Regarding my near-death experience. I chose to learn from it. The past is the past. It's what you choose to make of it. I chose to grow up and move forward. Become more of a man." Sebastian angrily answers Francois as he abruptly leaves the room. Francois closes and locks the door, he sleeps soundly through the night for the first time in a month.

Francois takes to eating his meals locked in his room. He gains weight, gets his color back. A box spring, bed frame, nightstand, and small lamp arrive over the next two weeks. He is up off the floor and finally warm enough to recover and not appear sickly.

Francois keeps his distance from Sergei and Sebastian while working in the kitchens and stables together. They learn to work amongst one another keeping a comfortable distance. He pulls his weight and slowly earns their trust. Little by little they learn to respect and trust one another's boundaries.

Happy Noel My Precious Kindle,

The winter weather has brought lots of snow. The nights are cold and lonely. I reach out for your warm embrace only to realize you're not there. Most of my day is consumed with shoveling snow off the walkways as well as removing snow from the roofs so as to keep them clear.

I dreamt last night that I was standing under the mistletoe awaiting your kiss, the soft scent of vanilla coming from your hair. The tinkle of your laughter ringing in my ears. I reach for you, only you're not there.

How are things at NYU, what is NYU like? What is New York City life like? It must be so alive. I wish we were sharing it together.

The snowflakes remind me of you. You're one of a kind beauty. Your hands so kind and gentle. Your heart is so strong and caring.

I wish I could be there in person to tell you just how much I care, how much I need you. How every day I grow stronger. One day I will be a better man. One day I will make you proud. Please be patient, Kindle.

Joyeux Noel,
Much Love,
Sebastian

Chapter 12

CHRISTMAS ARRIVES WITH RECORD BREAKING SNOWFALL. The Chalet is buried deep under snow and ice. With little else to do personal offerings become the business of days and nights. Requests for offerings coming in twenty-four hours a day. Between shoveling snow, clearing the snow off the roof, and pleasuring the guests there is little time for anything else. The week between Christmas and New Year's brings more record snowfall and even more record-breaking personal offering requests. Sebastian and Sergei are pleasuring four to six guests each day and six to seven a night. Some tip, most don't. The Chalet cooks enough food to feed an army and serves almost enough people to constitute a small army. For the first time in a long while even the indentured servants are fed more than they can possibly eat.

Christmas and New Year's is a time of celebration. A time of reflection as well as a time of resolutions. For the indentured servants, Christmas brings depression and resentment. The holiday season brings three suicides. Sebastian, Sergei, Francois and two new male servants, Edgar and Victor, are given burial detail. Digging graves is back-breaking work, the snow is deep, and the ground is frozen. Each body results in hours of grave digging and burial. No records are kept. The bodies are buried in the frozen ground and forgotten. After burying the bodies, exhausted and tired, Sebastian turns to leave. Sergei's soft singing stops him. He turns and listens to the unfamiliar hymn.

Sergei lays evergreen boughs on each grave, turns in silence, and walks back towards the servant's quarters. Sebastian, Edgar, Victor, and Francois follow in silence.

As Sebastian and Sergei are changing clothes and putting on their offering robes, Sebastian asks Sergei where he learned such a sad hymn.

"My father's first wife used to sing it at her infant daughter's grave. I don't know, I guess I learned it, memorized it. Just seemed appropriate."

"How did the little girl die?"

"Baby shaken syndrome. Her daughter was only a few weeks old when the young inexperienced nanny shook her to make her stop crying."

"What happened to the Nanny?"

"She was sold to the highest bidder." Sergei sadly answers.

Sebastian and Sergei finish dressing in silence. They exit the room together and head towards Corbett's office. It is just the beginning of a long exhausting night for Sergei and Sebastian. They are both reserved as personal offerings that night. Both will be presented to seven separate women before dawn. Edgar, Francois, and Victor will be presented as personal offerings as many times before dawn as Sergei and Sebastian. For Luscious Corbett business is good.

The sun rises and with it comes the sparkle of fresh fallen snow. Sergei enters the small room. Sebastian is already in bed sleeping. Sergei lies down and closes his eyes. They will be given three to four hours of rest before the alarm clocks ring and their work day begins.

The winter months pass slowly for the indentured servants. Harsh winter weather buries the Chalet under snow and ice. With little else to entertain the guests, the indentured servants are ordered to compete against one another. The competitions become their daily punishments. It's do as your ordered, or be locked in the freezing cold cellar with little to no food or water till the thaw of spring.

Chapter 13

SPRING ARRIVES IN EARLY MARCH. EXHAUSTED FROM COMPETING against one another all winter long, Sebastian is happy to return to his role as a chauffeur to wealthy clients. For Sergei, Edgar, Francois, and Victor, the arrival of spring is a welcome as well. Tending the fields and caring for the horses is a welcome change of pace. Francois moves out of his closet size room and bunks with Edgar and Victor in a small room identical to Sebastian's and Sergei's. The thaw of spring brings seven new female servants and four new male servants. Replacements for those sold or dead after the long harsh winter weather and competitions. Hunter Ryan's return to the resort leaves Sebastian rattled and sickened. Sebastian is ordered to present himself to Monsieur Corbett's office shortly after Hunter Ryan's arrival. Sebastian hasn't been with a man since Hunter Ryan's last visit. He's only had the pleasure of attending to female clientele over the long winter months. Some had smelled of vanilla and cinnamon, they had been gentle lovers. While others had smelled of expensive perfumes and had been fierce and abusive in the bedding chambers. The sting of a leather whip across his bare shoulders and ass while standing bent over grabbing his ankles still stung fresh in his memory.

Sebastian dresses in his silk green spring robes. He rubs peppermint oil into his hands and arms. Sebastian walks up to Monsieur Corbett's office. He knocks on the door and waits to be told he may enter.

Sebastian opens the door; his body is thrown to the floor. His feet and hands are bound with flex cuffs. A black hood is placed over his head and a pair of hands lift him off the floor. They carry him through the kitchen and out the private exit at the back of the kitchen. Sebastian's thrown into the trunk of a car. Panic sets in. What's happening, where are they taking him?

Sebastian rolls onto his back, his body aches. There's a second body in the trunk with him. The person next to him moans in pain. The car's engine roars to life, drives to the gates, and honks the horn twice. A few seconds later, the car pulls through the gates and makes an immediate right turn. The vehicle drives for what seems like an hour before slowing down and taking another right turn. The vehicle makes several more turns and comes to a final stop two and a half hours after leaving the Chalet. Sebastian's body is lifted out of the trunk of the car and placed in a standing position on a cold, frozen stone surface. His ankle restraints are cut off and he is instructed to walk forward. He is guided through the door of a privately owned cabin. The room is freezing. The restraints on his hands are cut off. Sebastian wants to rub his wrists but has no idea if rubbing his wrists would show a sign of weakness and result in his being punished. Sebastian lets his arms fall to his sides and awaits further orders. The door behind him opens and he can hear a second person shuffling in. The black hood covering his face is pulled off. Sebastian blinks there isn't much light in the room, he can sense the person to his left. Sebastian blinks his eyes again getting used to the low light. He looks to his left. Sergei stands next to him blinking his eyes as well waiting for his eyes to adjust. The person standing behind them cuts away Sergei's restraints and walks out the door behind them locking it before leaving. Sergei and Sebastian look around the room. Both are too scared to move or ask the other what's going on.

After several minutes pass, the door behind them unlocks and opens. A man and woman enter the room closing the door behind them and locking it. Sergei and Sebastian turn toward the man and woman.

"Do you speak and understand English?" the woman asks Sergei.

"Yes, mademoiselle." She nods and walks in front of Sebastian.

"And you speak and understand English as well?"

"Yes, mademoiselle." Sebastian answers.

"Good." The woman answers. "For the next three days, you will scrub and clean every inch of this cabin from top to bottom. You will be fed and allowed a small amount of time to rest. At night you will take care of our needs." The woman instructs Sergei and Sebastian. "You will not address us unless you are spoken to or asked a question. Do both of you understand?" The woman asks.

"Yes, Mademoiselle." Sebastian and Sergei answer in unison.

For the first two days, Sebastian and Sergei scrub and clean the cabin sixteen hours a day. They are given small amounts of food and water, as well as a few hours to rest and sleep. Sebastian, the stronger of the two, works hard to make up for Sergei who grows weaker by the hour. Something has made Sergei ill. Sebastian tries his best to cover up Sergei's illness. He hides it as best he can from his two new owners. He has no idea how long they will be kept at the cabin or if he and Sergei will ever see the Chalet again. Their new owners pay no attention to Sergei's illness. As long as Sergei is able to keep cleaning and scrubbing, they could care less about his physical well-being. Sebastian shares his food with Sergei hoping to give him the strength and energy he needs to keep working, to survive another hour, to survive another day.

After three long exhausting days, Luc returns to the cabin and restrains Sergei. The black hoods are placed back over their heads. Sergei is pale and exhausted. He can barely stand, much less walk, on his own. Luc instructs Sebastian to carry Sergei out to the car and place him in the trunk. Blinded wearing the black hood Sebastian walks slowly across the cabin. Sebastian steps out onto the frozen stone ground and gently places Sergei's body in the trunk of the car. Luc shoves Sebastian into the trunk next to Sergei, he restrains Sebastian's arms and ankles before slamming the trunk closed. Luc leaves Sebastian and Sergei restrained in the freezing cold trunk of the car with no food or water for three hours before leaving the Cabin and driving back to the Chalet. Sebastian struggles to push Sergei's body up against the back of the trunk. He positions his body next to Sergei's and huddles against Sergei's body. He prays he has enough body heat for the both of them.

Sergei is weak. He is burning up with a high fever. Sebastian carries Sergei back to their small room. Sebastian undresses Sergei and removes his own clothing. Sebastian turns the shower on and waits for the warm water to fall. Sebastian carries Sergei into the shower stall. Sebastian allows the warm water to fall over both of them while washing their bodies. The shower helps Sergei, and he is able to regain some of his strength. Francois gathers chips, sandwiches, and water from the servant's kitchen. Sebastian eats the chips and drinks some water. He allows Sergei to eat both of their sandwiches. Sebastian can wait till nightfall to sneak back into the kitchen and find more food for himself. Sergei on the other hand, he's not so sure about. Sebastian goes to find Jurai the head foreman. Sebastian invokes his right as Monsieur Corbett's eyes and ears and requests a private meeting with Monsieur Corbett.

Jurai returns an hour and fifteen minutes later. Sergei has fallen asleep and is barely able to breath. Sebastian is unable to revive him. Jurai restrains Sebastian's arms behind his back and escorts Sebastian up to the main guest house. Sebastian is told to stay in the parlor adjacent to Monsieur Corbett's office. Jurai walks Sebastian to the middle of the room and cuts off Sebastian's restraints. Jurai informs Sebastian that he is to stand at attention and await Monsieur Corbett. Ten minutes pass before Luscious Corbett arrives with Hunter Ryan and a young boy no older than fifteen. The boy is instructed to stand next to Sebastian.

"Sebastian, Jurai tells me that you wish to speak with me. I'm afraid that I still have a small matter of business to wrap up with Monsieur Ryan before he takes his leave. Would you please be so obedient as to keep young Emmett company while we finish our business? I'll handle your business afterwards." Corbett instructs Sebastian.

"Oui, Monsieur."

Hunter Ryan and Corbett exit the parlor and enter Corbett's private office. Twenty minutes later Hunter Ryan leaves the Chalet with two new young girls barely older than eleven or twelve. Young Emmett is left at the Chalet to serve Luscious Corbett's needs.

Corbett instructs Sebastian to follow him into his office and instructs Emmett to wait just outside the office door. Sebastian follows Corbett into his office, closes the door and walks to the center of the room. Sebastian stands at attention facing Corbett's desk.

"Sebastian, I'm told you have business with me?" Corbett tiredly inquires.

"Oui, Monsieur. It's my roommate, Sergei. I'm afraid he has fallen ill."

"What is wrong with Sergei?"

"When I left his side, he was unconscious, burning up with a fever. Jurai's assistant, Twink, was carrying him off to the infirmary."

Corbett picks up the phone and dials Dr. Maboob's private line. Sebastian turns to leave. "Did I give you permission to turn your back on me or to leave my office?" Corbett angrily growls.

Sebastian stops dead in his tracks. Cold fear washes over his entire body. A dagger of ice presses against his pounding heart. What on earth had he been thinking? Sebastian slowly turns, drops to his knees, crosses his ankles, and stares at the floor. "Non, Monsieur. I- I- I assumed you'd want privacy with the doctor. I- I'm sorry." Sebastian stutters staring at the floor. He knows that he has made a terrible mistake. A mistake he knows will not go unpunished. This will cost him dearly.

Corbett speaks briefly with Dr. Maboob before hanging up the phone.

"Sebastian, I'm afraid we still have some business to discuss." Corbett informs Sebastian.

"Monsieur?"

"Stop talking to the floor!" Luscious Corbett raises his voice and angrily stares at Sebastian. Sebastian raises his head and eyes from the floor.

"I'm sorry, Monsieur, merci, Monsieur."

"Sebastian, I have just purchased Emmett's contract from Hunter Ryan. Emmett's contract is an expensive contract so he will be bunking in yours and Sergei's room. A third bunk is being delivered to your room as we speak. You will assist Emmett with moving in. Help Emmett with his mattress and box spring. As I mentioned he is a seasoned and expensive contract so he will be given his bedding, nightstand, and lamp. Do you understand Sebastian?" Corbett barks angrily at Sebastian.

"Oui, Monsieur." Sebastian nervously stammers.

Corbett stares angrily at Sebastian, "Furthermore, you are to train Emmett over the next few days in the stables on how to properly care for my prize race horses. Emmett comes to us from a Swiss workhouse. Emmert knows hard work well. He has never worked or trained with live animals before. Do you understand Sebastian?"

"Oui, Monsieur."

"You may stand." Sebastian rises from the floor and stands perfectly still in the center of the room afraid to move.

Corbett opens his top desk drawer and removes the thick wooden paddle with holes drilled into it and a large leather whipping strap. Fear consumes Sebastian, he remembers the excruciating pain that paddle leaves in its wake.

"Sebastian, lower your pants and grab your ankles."

Hands shaking Sebastian unfastens the button on his jeans and lowers his pants. He bends over and grabs his ankles with shaking hands.

"Five strokes, you will thank me after each stroke."

"Oui, Monsieur."

"If you stumble, if you fall, if your hands touch the floor we start over. Understand?"

"Oui Monsieur."

The first stroke stings, "Un, Merci."

"Deux, Merci."

"Trois, Merci." the third stroke burns.

"Quatre, Merci." the fourth stroke takes his breath away. Tears caress his cheeks. Sebastian reaches deep inside himself and finds his inner strength. "Cinq. Merci, Monsieur."

"Stand, pull up your pants. Next time you won't be able to sit down for a week." Corbett barks.

Sebastian slowly stands, pulls up his jeans and buttons them with still shaking hands. He wipes the tears from his face.

Corbett walks to his desk, lays the paddle in the top desk drawer.

Corbett pushes a button on his phone and instructs Luc to bring young Emmett into his office. Corbett looks up from the phone. "Remove your shirt." Corbett growls. Hands still shaking Sebastian unbuttons and removes his shirt. Luc escorts Emmett into the office. Corbett instructs Emmett to stand facing Sebastian. Corbett hands the leather whip to Emmett, "A team is only as strong as its weakest member. Sebastian momentarily forgot his manners today. Five strokes for not being properly discharged from my office and five more for wrongful assumption." Corbett instructs Emmett.

Emmett raises the whip into the air and with an even downward stroke, the whip lands squarely in the middle of Sebastian's chest. Emmett raises the whip back into the air and with a second, even stroke it lands squarely across Sebastian's chest taking his breath away. Sebastian grits his teeth, and groans uncontrollably but refuses to cry out any louder. The third and fourth strikes land across his shoulders. The fifth across his chest again. Sebastian falls to his knees and shakes uncontrollably. Luc pulls him back up on his feet, grips his arms tightly by his sides and holds him upright. The sixth stroke lands squarely across his chest. Tears fall from Sebastian's eyes blinding him. He refuses to cry out. With the seventh and eighth stroke Sebastian's chest begins to burn and constrict. The ninth and tenth land across his shoulders. Sebastian groans as Luc releases his grasp. Sebastian wobbles but refuses to fall to the floor again. His breaths uneven Sebastian wipes the tears from his face with the back of his hand.

Sebastian doesn't blame Emmett for his pain. Sebastian's been in Emmett's shoes before, forced to whip another as their punishment. The whip falls to Emmett's side. Emmett steps forward and raises his arms to assist Sebastian. Sebastian shakes his head, Emmett steps back and lowers his arms. Corbett takes the whip from Emmett and places it back in his top desk drawer. "Emmett, you may leave, stand outside my office. Sebastian will show you to the stables and later to your living quarters. We still have some unfinished business. Sebastian will want to clean up before returning to the public eye." Corbett instructs Emmett.

Luc picks up Sebastian's shirt and tosses it in his face. "You may clean up in the kitchen's restroom. There is a bottle of aloe in the cabinet above the sink. Oh, and Sebastian, next time it'll be double the strokes." Luc coldly instructs him. Sebastian looks to Corbett for permission to leave the office. Corbett nods. Sebastian turns and walks towards the kitchen's bathroom. He turns the cold tap on and flushes his chest and shoulders with cold water. He fills his hands with water and lowers his face into the cool water. Sebastian reaches into the cabinet above the sink and pulls down the bottle of aloe. He coats the aloe onto his chest and shoulders, lowers his jeans and adds a little to his burning backside. He places the bottle back in the cabinet and puts his flannel shirt back on. Slowly he buttons his shirt feeling the uncomfortable itch as his shirt irritates his now burning chest and shoulders. Sebastian lowers his face into a handful of cold water one last time. He cleans up, takes a deep breath, and composes himself. He stares into the mirror above the sink, turns the cold water tap off, turns and leaves the small bathroom. He walks across the kitchen, through the double doors, and out into the main hallway. Sebastian instructs Emmett to follow him out of the main guest house and down to the stables. "I'm sorry, I tried not to keep hitting the same place over and over; it draws blood that way." Emmett nervously apologizes to Sebastian.

"It's alright, I'm not angry with you, Emmett. I momentarily forgot my place. Monsieur Corbett had a point to prove. Lesson learned. From here on we can only move forward." Sebastian and Emmett walk silently to the stables.

My Dearest Kindle,

I've been taught the painful lesson of humility. I've been taught the consequences of my actions. I've been taught that my actions affect not just me but those around me. Living at the orphanage, my actions only ever affected me. Now they affect all those around me.

How do I live with that knowledge; can I live with that knowledge? I've been a selfish S.O.B that has only ever thought of himself, that makes me a selfish, evil, arrogant man. How can you love someone like that, how can you love me?

How are your studies coming, is NYU as exciting and hard as we thought? Kindle, you must be so excited to be studying interior design in the real world, with real world applications.

Kindle reach for your dreams; excel as I know only you can. Don't make the same stupid, selfish mistakes that I made. Be kind and gentle, and never rule with an iron fist. Learn from your mistakes and move forward. Look to the future, never the past.

Much Love,
Sebastian

Chapter 14

SEBASTIAN WALKS PAST DR. MABOOB'S CAR. HE ANXIOUSLY looks around before sliding Kindle's letter through the open rear window and walks away. Emmett spots Sebastian and nervously catches up to him. "Where do I bunk down and clean up?" Emmett nervously asks.

"Follow me, I'll show you." Sebastian eye's Emmett.

"What?" Emmett asks.

"How old are you, Emmett?"

"Fifteen."

Sebastian's guess had been right.

"How long have you been a slave?" Sebastian asks.

"Since I was 11."

"I'm sorry. May I ask, why so young?"

"After my father passed away, his second wife became depressed, lonely, inconsolable. Eight months after my father's death my stepmother met an F1 driver. She fell madly in love, head over heels. Unable to locate my birth mother, she started leaving me with my aunt and uncle on my father's side of the family. She started stalking the F1 circuit. She became obsessed with her driver. She was stalking him from one race to the next. She visited me less and less. My aunt and uncle fell on hard times. I was sold to pay off their debts. I spent my first two years in Surrey, two more years in the servitude of Hunter Ryan in his workhouse in Switzerland. Now I'm here." Emmett explains.

"Do you think your birth mother or stepmother is searching for you?" Sebastian asks.

"At first I prayed every day that my birth mother was looking for me. Now, I just accept my fate. I hope that my real mother is happy and safe. My stepmother I couldn't care less. I have no idea where she is or even how to contact her."

"Sebastian, how old are you?"

"Eighteen."

"How long has it been for you?

"Two years."

"How were you pulled into this?"

"I made a lot of mistakes, piled up a rather large debt. Unable to pay off my debts, I allowed myself to be indentured to Monsieur Corbett. I'm in for life. I'll never be able to repay Monsieur Corbett for the medical bills I have incurred while serving here at the Chalet." Sebastian explains.

"Do you have any family out there searching for you?" Emmett asks.

"I'm not sure. I grew up in an orphanage. The sisters will think I ran away. I was dating a beautiful girl back home when I walked into this, eyes wide open with no way out. I hope she is looking for me but part of me hopes that she has moved on with her life. She deserves much more than I could ever give her."

Sebastian enters the servant's quarters and shows Emmett the dining area and the commons room. Both positioned at the far ends of the hallway. He shows him the laundry facilities located next to the commons room. Finally, he shows Emmett their small room. Sebastian assists Emmett with setting up his bunk. Each bunk is given its own wall. He places Emmett's bunk against the back wall between his and Sergei's beds. He moves his nightstand to the foot of his bed and places Emmett's between the two beds. Sebastian and Emmett take turns showering. Sebastian rubs more aloe onto his chest, shoulders, and backside. Emmett stands in the doorway guiltily watching. The soft scent of peppermint catches Emmett's attention as Sebastian applies the oil to his arms before changing into his offering robes.

"Why peppermint?" Emmett asks.

"It distracts me from the true purpose of what I must do." Sebastian softly answers.

"I'm sorry?"

"I'm a personal offering as well as a worker. Those that I serve aren't always my sexual preference." Sebastian awkwardly answers. "Dinner is served at the end of the hallway. I'll just grab a sandwich. I'm sorry I can't eat with you your first night. I'll introduce you to Sergei, our other roommate, in the next couple of days once he returns from the medical center. Try to get as much rest as possible. The hard work begins first thing tomorrow morning." Sebastian informs Emmett as he exits the room.

Sebastian reports to Corbett's office. Upon entering the office Sebastian is shocked to see that Hunter Ryan has returned to the Chalet. Corbett instructs Sebastian that he will be accompanying Monsieur Ryan to his private suite for the evening.

Aching, his head pounding, Sebastian gathers the blankets around his naked body and tries to sit up, the room spins. Hunter Ryan catches Sebastian as his body fails to hold his weight. Hunter Ryan lays Sebastian's body back against the pillows. "Don't fight it. It'll pass soon enough. It was intended to make things a little easier for you tonight. Guess I gave you a little too much." Hunter Ryan informs Sebastian. Sebastian sinks back into the pillows and closes his eyes. The drug pulls him back to sleep.

Sebastian rolls over and opens his eyes. He carefully tries sitting up again. "How long have I been out?" Sebastian asks. "It's only been a few hours. It's about 2 A.M." Hunter Ryan tells Sebastian. Sebastian wraps the blankets around his body and gets up. He gingerly walks towards the bathroom. Sebastian throws water on his face and lets it trickle down the front of his body. The cool water feels good against his irritated skin. “What happened to your butt and chest?” Hunter Ryan asks caressing Sebastian’s backside following him into the bathroom. “A punishment. I momentarily forgot my place. It won’t happen again. I should return to the servant’s quarters. I’m expected to train Emmett. I have to be up in four hours.” Sebastian explains. Hunter Ryan dismisses Sebastian and watches as he gingerly dresses and slowly exits the suite.

Sebastian returns to the servant’s quarters. He climbs into bed and stares at Sergei’s empty bunk. A feeling of fear and sadness consumes him. He stares at his new roommate and watches as his chest rises and falls with each breath. Emmett’s sleep is restless. Sebastian wonders if that is what it looks like when he is sleeping. Sebastian closes his eyes and welcomes the darkness over taking him.

Chapter 15

SEBASTIAN COMES TO THE FULL REALIZATION THAT IN THE unlikeliest of places while searching for Emmett's young profile amongst those reporting to breakfast, that he has found the family he has spent his entire life searching for. It isn't your typical family, more like a mixed family unit all experiencing the same horrific nightmare. While Sebastian is getting older, his family's getting younger. The girls serving breakfast couldn't be any older than 11 or 12, the boys washing dishes in the back, no older than 13. When Sebastian had come to live at the compound he had been among the youngest. When had things changed so drastically? When had he stopped paying attention?

Sebastian notices Emmett's young profile sitting in the middle of the room. Sebastian piles a plate with cold eggs and ham, two stale muffins, and grabs a mug of cold java. He walks to the middle of the cafeteria and gingerly sits down next to Emmett. "Watching hours of pornography will grow to become tedious but pay attention. It'll teach you what the clientele expects of you. Don't fall asleep. They'll make an example of you, strip you and whip you in front of everyone. It will all be over in a few hours. Just don't fall asleep." Sebastian heavily emphasizes his last statement.

"How long will we be expected to watch porn?" Emmett asks.

"Three to four hours a day your first week. Just make it through the humiliation of public sex acts during your training. Find your safe place in the dark recesses of your mind and visit it as often as possible. It's all over in a week. After that you only have to perform when offered up as a private offering. I'm your mentor, so to speak. If you have any questions just ask. I'll explain what I can and help you as best as I'm humanly able to." Sebastian explains to Emmett.

"You will think you're going crazy. You'll cry, you'll puke, just try to do these things in private. You will be shown no pity, no mercy from our captors. It's all you'll be able to do to differentiate reality from nightmare. Sergei and I will help you as best we can. Just live long enough to complete all the training and in the end, you'll find something to cling to that will keep you smack dab in the middle of reality. Just find your safe place and cling to it. Cling to it like your life depends on it. Visit it as often as needed. Do you understand, Emmett?" Sebastian asks. Emmett quietly nods and searches his mind for any memory of a happy time or place where he felt safe.

Sebastian walks Emmett to the other end of the hallway. Sebastian pats Emmett on the shoulder and leaves him at the commons room entrance for his first day of training with the other new recruits.

The first week passes slowly for Emmett. For Sebastian it's long and excruciating. Sergei returns mid-week feeling stronger and healthier. Their small room becomes crowded. Sergei and Sebastian mentor Emmett as best they can, giving him his privacy when needed and support when needed most.

THE TRUST OF THE INNOCENT IS THE LIAR'S MOST USEFUL TOOL.

- STEPHEN KING

THERE WAS SUCH A SMALL AMOUNT OF HUMANITY THAT I EXPERIENCED IN PROSTITUTION. THE MOST MICROSCOPIC SPECS I SAW OR EXPERIENCED WERE FRAIL. NOT NEARLY STRONG ENOUGH TO LIGHT A SPARK OF HOPE FOR A LIFE OUTSIDE OF PROSTITUTION. NEVER ENOUGH HUMANITY TO ALLOW THE INNER ME TO SEEP OUT.

— CHRISTINE "CLARITY" MCDONALD

IT IS FOR EVERYONE TO MAKE THEIR VOICES HEARD. TO SAY HUMAN TRAFFICKING MUST END.

— K.R. RAVINDRAN
WORLD SUMMIT ON ENDING SEXUAL EXPLOITATION

Chapter 16

SEBASTIAN WORKS AS A CHAUFFEUR ON THE WEEKENDS AND IN the fields with Sergei and Emmett during the week. Most nights, Sebastian, Emmett and Sergei are amongst the more popular private offerings. They service as many as three to five clients each night. Most are only interested in sexual acts, but some like to take pictures or record their humiliation. Bent over the chair, Sebastian faces the camera as told. Sebastian prays that Kindle will never witness his humiliation. It embarrasses Sebastian to think that Kindle would ever see these photos or videos. It would kill him if she ever knew the truth. With each thrust Sebastian gasps for breath. Unable to disassociate himself from the harsh reality of rape Sebastian closes his eyes and cries out in pain. As a final act of domination they whip the bare soles of his feet.

Unable to stand, much less walk, Sebastian collapses to the floor. His feet burn, his legs violently shake as he tries to stand. Sebastian crawls to the bathroom and grasps the rim of the toilet, crying as he violently hurls what little he has in his stomach. Dizzy and unable to stand, he curls up on the floor and waits while his captors pack up their cameras and equipment. They leave him naked curled up in the fetal position alone and shivering on the bathroom floor. Upon hearing the last of the crew leave Sebastian crawls out of the bathroom to the main room and finds his robes and briefs thrown in a pile in the corner of the room. He gently pulls his briefs on and covers himself with his robes. He reaches for the phone and calls the servants quarters.

Sergei and Emmett arrive a short time later and carry Sebastian back to the servant's quarters. Sergei wraps his blanket around Sebastian. Emmett and Sergei sit on either side of Sebastian and wait for him to open up. Sebastian shakes and rocks in place as he stares at the far wall.

Sebastian's eyes grow heavy. He lies back against the cold stone wall and closes his eyes. His body goes limp against the wall. Emmett and Sergei climb off the bed and position Sebastian's body comfortably in his bed. Emmett covers him up and lifts his head placing his pillow beneath his head. Sergei shuts the lights off and both young men collapse into their beds. Sebastian is restless for the first few hours. He moans in pain as he restlessly sleeps. The early morning hours approach, Sebastian's body settles down and peaceful sleep comes at last.

Sunday morning is met by hurricane winds and rain. The servants are awarded a few extra hours to themselves. Emmett and Sergei leave Sebastian in his bed to peacefully sleep a few extra hours. They quietly straighten up and clean the room for its weekly inspection by Jurai and his young assistant, Twink. They save a small plate with two peanut butter and honey sandwiches for Sebastian to eat after he wakes up.

The weather grows worse as the day gets later. The servants clean their rooms, the common room, and the communal shower room and dining hall. They stand outside their rooms along the wall as Jurai and Twink inspect and grade the cleanliness of each room and communal areas. Pleased with their hard work and cleanliness they are given the rest of the afternoon to catch up on sleep. Time most of them haven't had in several months if ever. Sebastian wakes up, showers, and finds the plate with the two peanut butter and honey sandwiches. He quietly eats and gulps down two glasses of water. He still isn't ready to talk about being raped and whipped in front of cameras and photographers. He heads to the stables. He feeds and cares for the horses. He finds peace in his work, a subtle calm.

Sebastian lies back in the hay and stares up into the rafters. He thinks about killing himself but finds he doesn't have the strength or will to follow through. Sebastian pictures Kindle's sweet, innocent face. He pictures her laughing at him stumbling with his English vocabulary in school. Kindle standing in front of the Eiffel Tower wind blowing through her hair. Kindle at a sidewalk café enjoying a cup of English Tea. Always so beautiful, always laughing or smiling. Sebastian never saw Kindle sad or scared. She was always happy and always smelled of vanilla; God how he misses her.

Sebastian hears Francois enter the stables. He watches as Francois climbs up into the rafters and disappears into a small dark alcove. That's where Francois finds solace. The place where he feels safest. No wonder no one has ever been able to find him. Sebastian had never noticed the alcove before. Never knew it existed. For two years he's been working in the stables on a daily basis. How had he never noticed it before?

Sebastian works the kitchens that evening during dinner, cooking and serving food. Sebastian eats a small amount of food himself before showering and changing into his offering robes. Emmett and Sergei join Sebastian in the main hall of the Chalet. Emmett and Sergei look at one another and pass the same concerned glances in Sebastian's general direction. Sebastian is pale and shaken. Not quite all there. There is little they can do for him, so they just do their best to keep an eye on him throughout the night. From one suite to the next. One client after another they watch out for Sebastian in the hallways.

Sebastian's night is easier than his previous. Tonight, the clients are looking for sex and nothing more. Sebastian finds his way easily to the Opera House four times that night. Sebastian's services end a little after two in the morning. Sebastian arrives back at the servant's quarters tired and aching. He finds Emmett in the shower. Sergei is still servicing his last client.

Sebastian waits for Emmett to finish showering before taking his turn. As he gets out of the shower, Sebastian hears Sergei's return. Sebastian gets into bed and waits till Sergei is showered and ready for bed. As the last of the lights are turned off, Sebastian rolls over in his bed and faces Sergei's and Emmett's bed. Sebastian thinks about how to word his feelings. "Thank you for not pushing me or asking me a lot of questions. It isn't easy to talk about." he pauses and shifts uncomfortably from under his thin blanket. "The clients had cameras and video equipment. I can't even begin to explain what was expected of me, or the pain and humiliation." Sebastian rolls over and faces the wall. Tears well up in his eyes. He closes his eyes and tries to push the memory away.

"You'd have done the same for us. We watch out for one another. We are brothers." Sergei answers.

"You both trained and mentored me. We are all in this together." Emmett answers.

Sebastian wakes up early and grabs a cup of java for once it is hot instead of cold. He walks to the end of the hall and out the door. He watches as the sun rises. This is his favorite part of the day. Quiet, peaceful, no one around to remind him that he is anything but free. For a few moments he forgets that he is an indentured servant.

Sebastian heads back inside and changes into his chauffeur's uniform. He walks to the garage and checks out the remote key to the Bentley. Sebastian wipes the car down, climbs in, and drives up to the main guest house. Sebastian is chauffeuring Nicolas Skye this week. Nicolas is an investment banker conducting business in Paris for the week. Sebastian parks the car and walks to the servant's entrance. He lets himself in and reports to Monsieur Corbett's office for his GPS wrist monitor.

Nicolas Skye is a generous man with a healthy appetite. Monsieur Skye enjoys eating at the same establishment each morning. Nicolas Skye speaks seven fluent languages. French, German, Spanish, Russian, Mandarin, Italian, and English. He conducts business all over the world. Sebastian listens to his conversations as he conducts business in seven different languages on three different smartphones all at the same time. "Sebastian, how about two orders of Eggs Benedict, buttered toast, and orange juice." Nicolas Skye asks.

"Oui, Monsieur."

They are greeted by a beautiful young female server; she smells of fresh picked roses. Nicolas orders their morning meal. "deux commandes Eggs Benedict, toasts beurres, de jus d'orange."

Sebastian is reminded of the simple joy of eating hot food with generous company.

"Merci, Monsieur Skye."

"Votre accueil, Sebastian."

Sebastian guiltily eats his delicious hot breakfast. His fellow indentured servants will be eating cold bowls of stale cereal this morning. Sebastian is once again reminded of the value of enjoying the simple things in life. Nicolas Skye is a generous man, but not a talkative man outside of his business transactions. Sebastian enjoys the silence, less chance of having to explain that he's a slave not used to being treated as an equal. With Monsieur Skye's generous tips, Sebastian is able to buy new undershirts and briefs as well as new razors, shaving cream, soap, shampoo, and toothpaste for himself and his roommates for the next month. Sebastian spends most of the next week accompanying Nicolas Skye to law firms and banks. He is treated to breakfast each morning. Sebastian feels guilty because he knows that back at the servant's quarter's his roommates and other servants are eating day old food from the main house dining facilities. Cold eggs and ham, soggy crepes or waffles. At least the milk and juice are always fresh and cold.

Sebastian enjoys his time working as a chauffeur. He can pretend for a little while that he is a normal person with a normal job. The bulky GPS monitor is the only reminder that he isn't a free man with a normal chauffeur's job. Sebastian makes several trips to the airport picking up and delivering guests, as well as picking up and delivering packages for Monsieur Corbett. Sebastian has learned over time to never ask what is in the packages that he picks up or delivers. Sebastian thinks about running, escaping, but then he thinks about how the others would be tortured and punished for his actions. If he goes to the police, he doesn't know which ones to trust or which ones will call Monsieur Corbett and turn him back over to his captor. He has no idea which precinct Kindle's father works at. His contract is iron-clad, there is no way out for him except by death and Sebastian isn't ready to die just yet. He has no idea how to remove the GPS device strapped to his wrist. It takes a special electronic key to remove the device from his wrist that can only be found in Monsieur Corbett's office.

Hunter Ryan returns to the compound monthly and each time he inquires into Sebastian's contract. Each time Hunter Ryan's offer is turned down. Luscious Corbett has invested a great deal of time and euros into Sebastian's contract and has no intention of selling or trading him for any amount of euros. Even if he wished to sell Sebastian's contract, Hunter Ryan wouldn't have enough money to afford Sebastian's contract. For now Sebastian is destined to remain at Luscious Corbett's Chalet.

Sebastian and Francois find refuge in the stables. They learn to ignore one another's movements. They each find their own peace and solitude in a different way. The peace that Sebastian finds grooming and caring for the horses allows him to feel human for a few hours each week.

My Dearest Kindle,

I have found a family in the least likely of places I would have ever thought to look... It's not your everyday family but more of a blended foster family. It's like having brothers and sisters I barely knew a year ago and now can't imagine living without.

I have found peace in my work with the horses. They never judge, much less discriminate against anyone. I have been angry for far too long; I have only thought of myself for most of my life. Why was I so ignorant, so childish, so selfish?

I'm not sure how much longer I have in this life, but I don't plan on wasting what little time I have left. I'm going to be more supportive and caring with the time I have left.

Kindle, I want to tell you about Sergei and Emmett, they are the best friends any man could ever ask for. They have learned my deepest darkest fears; they have taught me how to overcome my own personal fears. When I have no one else I can turn to, I turn to them. They have never turned me away. They have gone out of their way to ease my pain, ease the hollow emptiness. They have forgone sleep just to keep me company, to keep me from doing something rash and stupid. Without their friendship I fear that I would have lost the ability to trust anyone.

Sophie is the youngest. She cries a lot because she's so small and scared. I want to protect her but have no idea how to protect her from that which I'm unable to stand up to myself. It's hard to explain, but there are dangers that even scares me.

I have learned to live amongst my enemies; I share the same hidden secret as my arch nemesis. We both find refuge in the same place only we have learned to give space to one another. I have given up on hate, just not comfortable in his company. A year ago, I wanted to kill him, now I feel only pity and empathy for him. One day I'll explain what that means. One day I'll have to explain all of this so that you'll understand.

How are your studies at NYU? Your student life must be so exciting. I've told my new-found brothers and sisters all about you, about how you're going to rock this world with your amazing interior designs, how one day you will change the world we live in for the better of all mankind.

Kindle, you're an amazing woman don't you ever forget that, because I know that I will never forget what an amazing person you have been to me. How are your parents? Your patience, your kindness, your compassion. I love you for who you are, never change that about yourself.

Much Love,
Sebastian

Chapter 17

KINDLE RAINES STANDS OUTSIDE HER FATHER'S OFFICE. Christian Raines is a ruggedly handsome man. He's tall, muscular, and strong. Kindle has her father's eyes as well as his strength. She hugs the shoebox to her chest. She had been so stupid not to tell her father about the letters. When they first started arriving, she hadn't been concerned, but lately the letters have changed. The letters have taken on a darker tone frightening Kindle. She has to tell her father. She has to show him the letters. All of them. Especially Sebastian's last letter.

Kindle knocks on the door. Inspector Raines looks up from his desk. He's surprised but delighted to see his daughter. "Everything alright, honey? I didn't forget a lunch date, or something did I?" Raines asks his daughter.

"No, papa, I should have called before stopping by unannounced. Are you busy? I can wait if I've interrupted anything important." Kindle answers smiling mischievously at her father.

Inspector Rains stands up. He shoves the file he is reading into his top desk drawer and invites his daughter into his office. Christian walks around to the front of his desk and embraces his daughter. "I'm hungry, how about you? Would you care to join me for a bite to eat?" Christian asks his daughter.

"Sure, papa, but there's something I need to tell you. Something I need to show you."

"Sure, honey. Over a bite to eat. You're looking too skinny. Are they feeding you at college? How long are you home for?" Christian asks his daughter.

"A week, Papa. The food at NYU is quite good but sometimes I miss mama's cooking." Kindle tells her father laughing. "But papa, there really is something I need to tell you. Something I need to show you," she urgently starts to explain again.

"Can you bring it with you? I'm starving." Rains asks his daughter as he escorts her out of his office towards the café across the street.

"Sure, papa, whatever you say." Kindle laughs.

Kindle links her arm around her father's arm like when she was a little girl and follows him across the street. She takes a seat across from her father. They get a table that is off to the side away from the commotion of the main dining area.

"What would you like to order?" Raines asks his daughter.

Kindle loves eating at this little pub. She has been having lunch with her father at this pub since she was just a little girl no older than three or four. Kindle has always loved the grilled chicken Caesar salad. "Je voudrais la salade de Ceasar avec poulet grillé et un cola."

"Je voudrais le tilapia grille, asparagus et un verre d'eau," Christian Raines orders next.

Kindle waits till the server delivers theirs drinks and leaves before pulling the lid off the shoe box on her lap and sitting it on the table in front of her father. "Papa, I should have told you about these a long time ago. At first, I thought Sebastian had joined the Peace Corps, that he had gone to one of those third world countries to make a better man of himself. The letters come from here in Paris and sometimes Belgium. I contacted the local Peace Corps office and asked if Sebastian had signed up with them. They have no record of his joining the Peace Corp. Next, I looked into his having joined the military, but again there is no record of his having joined any branch of the military. Once he left the orphanage there is no record of him. Papa, I fear he is in trouble and I don't know how to help him." Kindle finally breathes and waits for her father's response.

Inspector Raines lifts the small box off the table and looks inside. Neatly stacked and tied with a lavender ribbon are all of Sebastian's letters. Oldest on the bottom, newest on top. The soft scent of peppermint comes from the letters inside the box.

As their meals arrive, Inspector Raines sits the box on the empty chair next to him. Christian pulls the letters out one at a time and reads them while eating his grilled tilapia. He sips his water. Kindle eats and patiently waits for her father's response. She feels guilty for not having shared the letters with her father when Sebastian had first disappeared.

Christian Raines understands his daughter's concern. He reads all of Sebastian's letters. The letters also begin to confirm his worst fears. Sebastian's last letter concerns him the most. Christian Raines understands why Kindle feels the need to finally share Sebastian's private letters with him. Raines folds the last letter and returns it to its place in Kindles shoe box.

"I won't lie and tell you that I didn't know about these letters. Your mother has been photographing the envelopes for the last few years. We wondered what the letters consisted of. I must admit we were disappointed when you didn't feel you could share them with us or tell us about them. Using the postmarks from the photographed letters I have expanded my search to include Belgium. Now with these letters I can cross reference the names he mentions in his last letter with other missing person's reports. None of the names stand out. Which means if they are missing then they're not getting a whole lot of attention or recognition." Inspector Raine's explains to his daughter.

"Papa, you have to find him, you have to help him. You promised me when he first turned up missing that you'd do everything in your power to find him and bring him back home." Kindle begs her father.

"Kindle, I have never given up on Sebastian's case, I have made thousands of inquiries and will continue to investigate his disappearance. I won't stop till I have all the answers I need to bring him home. This I promise you. These letters will help, thank you for finally sharing them." Christian Raines explains to his daughter.

Kindle walks back with her father to his office. Inspector Raine's makes digital as well as photocopies of the letters to add to Sebastian's already existing file in his top desk drawer. Christian Raine's is pleased to have his daughter home from school for a week but he really has to get back to work. Christian walks with Kindle back out to the parking lot. He hugs and kisses his daughter goodbye. He promises to be home early tonight for dinner. Kindle leaves and drives back to her parent's house. She hadn't called to say she was coming home. She had wanted to surprise her mom.

Inspector Raines returns to his office and starts investigating the names of the boys and the girl mentioned in the letter with any known missing persons files. He rereads the letters and worries about Sebastian's safety. Christian Raines is impressed by his daughter's investigation into the Peace Corps and military. She has saved him time as well as several phone calls. He often wondered at times if his daughter wouldn't make a great investigator someday. But she has her own dreams and a knack for interior design. He could never ask his daughter to give up her love of interior design. He would never take that pleasure from his only daughter. He is proud of her hard work and high marks in school. Kindle's on the A/B honor roll at NYU. Kindle is well on her way to becoming a huge success, the female version of America's Nate Berkus and Jeremiah Brent.

Inspector Raines wraps his work up early and informs his chief that his daughter's home from NYU and that he's heading home for an early dinner with his family. Inspector Raines wishes his chief a happy weekend and promises to be back bright and early Monday morning. He pulls out of the parking lot and heads home to enjoy the weekend with his wife and daughter.

Driving home Inspector Raines makes plans for horseback riding and hiking with his wife and daughter. Maybe even find time for a quick trip into the city to visit the Eiffel Tower. No matter how old Kindle gets she always enjoys visiting the Eiffel Tower. Maybe there would be time for a quick trip to the Arc de Triomphe at Place de L'Etoile at the top of the Champs-Elysees. Kindle always enjoys touring the City of Paris and acting like a tourist. She can spend hours snapping photos of anything and everything. Never knowing where she might get her next great inspiration or design idea.

Chapter 18

SEBASTIAN SHAKES FROM HEAD TO TOE. THE COLD WATER feels like needles piercing his skin. It felt great six hours ago after Luc had whipped him on his chest, back, and ass thirty strokes each. A grand total of ninety with the largest cruelest whip in his arsenal. But six hours later, restrained and on his knees his body feels only pain. He prays for the freezing cold water to numb him, but no such luck. The water has progressively gotten colder over the last six hours. Six hours kneeling in the shower the tiles digging into his kneecaps. The circulation in his hands and feet cut off by the tightness of his restraints. The only parts of his body to mercifully go numb.

Sebastian plays the day's events over and over in his head. Six hours is a long time to mull over the accident. No matter what choice he'd made there had been no way to stop the other vehicle from plowing into the Bentley. Sebastian had been late arriving at Paris Nord Train Station. From the train station Sebastian had been caught in traffic causing him to arrive late at Charles de Gaulle Airport to pick up Luc. He was already being lectured and threatened with a harsh punishment for being late when the speeding car plowed into them, T-boning the Bentley and pushing them into a retaining wall. There had been no way to avoid the speeding vehicle or to save the Bentley. It had taken all his strength to force the door open and pull Luc out of the back of the Bentley. They were both uninjured except for a few minor bumps and bruises.

Monsieur Corbett hadn't seen it that way. Luscious Corbett blamed Sebastian for running late, leading to Sebastian's being in the wrong place at the wrong time. Monsieur Corbett had accused Sebastian of jack rabbiting, of endangering the Chalet's business, and of trying to kill his only son. His only living heir.

Eight long hours and the water finally cuts off. Sebastian's restraints are cut free. Sebastian's body screams in pain as he tries to stand. Luc shoves him on his side and steps out of the small glass shower stall locking the door behind him as he leaves. Sebastian's punishment is far from over. Sebastian lies in the fetal position unable to move. Every fiber of his body aching and throbbing. Sebastian bites the inside of his mouth and concentrates on the new pain. He won't cry, he won't give Monsieur Corbett the satisfaction. For two long painful hours Sebastian lies on the floor shivering. Sebastian whimpers as the water turns back on. Sebastian slowly, painfully rolls his body towards the small corner in the back of the shower. The water on the floor of the shower slowly begins to warm up. Sebastian slowly rolls back under the steady stream of water and sure enough he feels warm water cascade over his aching body. Slowly his body heats back up. Throughout the day the water switches between warm and cold. Sebastian's body seizes up and aches with each hour of cold. His body releases and finds peace with each hour of warmth. Unable to sleep for fear of drowning, Sebastian pulls himself up to a sitting position and leans against the back glass wall.

Twenty-four hours pass before Luc returns and drags Sebastian's water soaked, wet naked body out of the shower stall. Sebastian stands in the middle of Corbett's office dripping large drops of water onto Corbett's office floor. Luc hands Sebastian a towel to wrap around his midsection. Sebastian stands shakily, barely able to hold his own body weight. Sebastian stands at attention, his hands by his side. Luscious Corbett stares at Sebastian, gets up, and walks around the desk. He slowly walks in circles around Sebastian's wet shivering body. Sebastian stares at the wall behind Monsieur Corbett's desk. He dares not speak nor make eye contact.

Fear consumes Sebastian's mind and body. Luscious returns to his desk and sits back down. Sebastian spends the rest of the day standing at attention staring at his reflection in the newly placed mirror on the wall behind Corbett's desk. Sebastian fights to hold his own body weight up, legs shaking from pain and fatigue. Early evening, he is given a small cut of cheese and a dinner roll along with a small bottle of water. That night Sebastian is given a clean pair of briefs and an offerings robe. Luc hands Sebastian a small bath pillow and a towel to use as a blanket. Sebastian is told that he will be spending the night on the bathroom floor. Sleep if he can, tomorrow he will be given a permanent place to stand and stare at the wall. For the next five days Sebastian is given bread and water in the morning along with a clean set of robes and briefs. He stands in the same spot and studies the same crack in the wall. In the evening he is given cheese, bread, and a small bottle of water. Each night he is locked in the bathroom and forced to sleep on the floor. Sebastian uses the tap in the bathroom to refill his water bottle throughout the night. In total he spends a week sleeping on the floor of the bathroom before he is allowed to return to his small room with Emmett and Sergei. He relives the nightmare as he tells Emmett and Sergei where he has been for the past week. Sebastian takes his first hot shower and eats his first warm meal in a week. Again, he worries about how young most of the servants appear. Sebastian, Emmett, Francois and Sergei appear to be the oldest in the group. Sebastian eats slowly and enjoys not having to eat while standing up. He clears his plate and cup and returns them to the dish washing rack. Sebastian walks down the hall past his small room and heads outside for the first time in a week. The sun is setting, a cool refreshing breeze blowing across his face. The scent of fresh cut hay blows on the breeze along with the scent of fresh cut grass. Sebastian watches as mother nature paints the sky with all her brilliance. It's magnificent. Sebastian's grateful to be as close to freedom as his servitude allows. Sebastian notices Francois standing off to the side staring up at the sunset, like a painting in the sky. Like Sebastian, it's the few moments of peace that they both cherish the most. Sebastian turns to leave.

"Sebastian?" Francois quietly calls out. Sebastian turns. "Yeah." It would be rude to just ignore him. The sisters had taught him better manners than that.

"Je suis desole."

"What are you sorry for?" Sebastian asks.

"Everything, I never understood until I was forced into your world. I didn't understand how much I was taking from you. What it was I was destroying in you. I mean I knew, but I just didn't understand entirely." Francois answers. He turns to leave and give Sebastian his privacy.

"Don't leave, s'il vous plait, I could use the company. It's been a long week. Stay, talk s'il vous plait. I've missed human companionship." Sebastian begs Francois.

Francois leans nervously against the wall and waits for Sebastian to speak first. Sebastian opens his mouth but doesn't know where to start. "Francois, have you always lived here. I mean did you grow up here at the Chalet?"

"I didn't grow up here. Not exactly. My parents died when I was 13, that's when I came to live at my uncle's Chalet."

"Where did you live before here?"

"Avignon."

"Oh, where is Avignon?"

"Avignon is about five hundred eighty kilometers Southeast of Paris."

"You haven't gotten out much, have you?" Francois asks.

"I grew up in a small orphanage just outside of Paris. We only left the orphanage to attend school and church services. What is Avignon like? Do you miss it?"

"Avignon is an old kind of beautiful. It sits on the banks of the Rhone River. Sometimes I miss it but most of all I miss my parents."

"What were your parents like? I don't remember my parents."

"Mon pere was a professor of law at The University of Avignon. Ma mere was a nurse at the local medical clinic."

"How long did you live at the orphanage?" Francois asks.

"As long as I can remember. I was about three or four days old when I was delivered to the sisters."

"Do you know anything about who your parents were? Did your mother die giving birth to you?"

"Non. She gave birth and just left me at the hospital. I don't know who my parents were or why they just left me at the hospital unclaimed."

"Where did you live before coming here after you left the Orphanage?"

"The orphanage is the only home I've ever had. I was on the streets for a few days before coming to the Chalet."

"Oh, I'm sorry. You have never experienced life, have you?" Francois asks.

"Non not really."

Sebastian and Francois lean against the building in silence. Francois tries to imagine going through life never knowing who your parents were. Never knowing who you are or where you came from. From the orphanage to slavery. Never truly tasting freedom. What kept him fighting for a chance to live? Francois had the memories of his parents to keep him strong. What kept Sebastian strong?

"Sebastian, do you think we're born good or evil, or do you think it's a life choice?" Francois asks.

"I'm sorry, Francois but honestly I believe it's a life choice."

"Sebastian, I'm so sorry. I fear that I made all the wrong choices. I tortured you and the other servants because it was what was expected of me. I was an angry kid when I arrived at my uncle's Chalet. I allowed myself to be blinded, to be molded. My parents would be so ashamed of the man I've allowed myself to become. I'm not making excuses. I'm just trying to explain what I mean. You must hate me."

"I used to hate you. I used to resent you. Now, I don't know. It's all so tiring. The need for companionship outweighs the hate. Thank you for hanging out, for trying to be honest. It's a small step towards forgiveness." Sebastian explains.

Sebastian smiles at Francois and turns to enter the building. "Sebastian, merci, I'm not perfect. Far from it, but I'll try to be a friend if you'll allow me to." Francois follows Sebastian into the servant's quarters. Sebastian considers Francois' offer. He turns and answers "We start from scratch. The past is forgotten. Understood?"

"Oui. Good night, Sebastian"

"Goodnight, Francois."

Sebastian returns to his small room and falls into bed. Sebastian worries about his never ending punishment that begins tomorrow morning. Unable to hold his eyes open any longer Sebastian lets go of his fears and falls deeply, soundly to sleep in a soft warm bed for the first time in a week.

Chapter 19

SEBASTIAN FACES THE LONGEST PUNISHMENT TO DATE SINCE arriving at the Chalet. Each morning begins with his picking out a belt, whip, strap, or paddle. Handing it to Luc or Monsieur Corbett. He unbuttons his shirt or fully strips down depending on that morning's choice. He either grabs his ankles, drops to his knees or stands at attention. Most mornings he receives 10 to 20 strokes or lashes across his back, chest or his naked arse. Each morning, he has to thank them and wait for permission to get dressed and leave the office. He works in the fields during the day and in the kitchens in the evenings. Sebastian works as a personal offering every night. By the end of the summer Sebastian is 23 pounds lighter, struggling with headaches, and experiencing dizzy spells. Dr. Maboob's arrival is almost welcoming except it adds even more debt to his already ever-growing deficit to Monsieur Corbett's Chalet.

On the first day of the fall equinox, Monsieur Corbett grants Sebastian the reprieve he has waited all summer to hear. Sebastian's punishment is over, and Sebastian earns his first day off in 68 days. Sebastian celebrates by collapsing and sleeping for 16 straight hours.

Autumn brings cooler weather and bright colorful leaves. Crisp autumn air and the smell of roasted chestnuts and roasted pumpkin seeds.

Autumn also brings the return of Hunter Ryan. Sebastian showers and dresses in his maroon robes, he walks up to Monsieur Corbett's office. Corbett informs him that Luc will be escorting him to Hunter Ryan's suite this evening.

Sebastian nervously follows two steps behind Luc as they walk in silence towards Hunter Ryan's suite. At the top of the stairs Luc turns and pulls Sebastian off to the left instead of to the right towards Hunter Ryan's suite. Sebastian's heart races. Fear consumes him. Luc pulls Sebastian down a small dark corridor and turns to face Sebastian. "You work with Francois? How is he?" Luc whispers.

Sebastian stares at Luc in shock. Slowly his heart resumes beating normally. "Oui, we work in the fields and kitchens together." Sebastian nervously whispers back.

"You two talk?"

"Oui, Monsieur."

"How is he?"

"He's accepted his new life."

"Is he safe?"

"His life is no longer in danger if that's what you are asking. Oui, Francois is safe."

"You two are friends?"

"We're learning to trust one another. I guess you could say we're friends."

"Would you give him something from me? It'll give him some peace and solace."

Sebastian studies Luc's face. He begins to wonder if he can trust Luc.

"I have given you little reason to trust me, if Luscious finds out that Francois has been given this token back it will trace back to me and only me. I'm the one charged with the burden of withholding it from Francois. Francois would only be able to get this from me as far as Luscious is concerned." Luc explains to Sebastian.

Luc hands Sebastian a small, silver, ladies compact. Sebastian studies it. It's not expensive but well-worn like someone had held onto it and cherished it.

"Open it, it'll help you understand." Luc instructs Sebastian.

Sebastian opens the compact. Inside are two sets of pictures. The first picture is of a man and woman that look an awful lot like Francois. The second picture is of an older couple, most likely Francois grandparents. The family resemblance is strong. Sebastian closes the compact and nods at Luc. "I'll deliver it to him in the morning. We are both scheduled to work the breakfast shift tomorrow morning."

"Sebastian, I know you were not trying to kill me earlier this year. Thank you for pulling me out of the wreckage." Luc turns and heads towards Hunter Ryan's suite. Sebastian shoves the compact deep into the pockets of his robes and walks two steps behind Luc to Hunter Ryan's suit. Luc knocks twice on the door; he turns and leaves Sebastian standing by himself just outside the door to Hunter Ryan's suit.

Sebastian enters Hunter Ryan's suit and drops to his knees, crosses his ankles and unhooks his robe allowing the silk material to drop to the floor. Hunter Ryan offers Sebastian a glass of scotch. Sebastian drinks it savoring the warmth as it hits his throat. He sits the glass down and crawls on his hands and knees to the bedroom. Climbs on the bed and assumes the position. The scotch flows through Sebastian's system warming and loosening up his muscles. Monsieur Ryan has no complaints that night. For three hours Sebastian digs deep to find his memories of the afternoon at the Louvre, his memories of the evening out at the Opera de la Bastille.

Sebastian opens his eyes. The room is still dark. Hunter Ryan is snoring on the other side of the bed. Sebastian sits up and looks around the room. Slowly his recollection comes back to him. Sebastian gets up, walks to the bathroom, cleans up and pulls his robes back on. The cool metal of the compact in his pocket reminds him of the promise made earlier that night. Sebastian pulls the compact out and opens it up. He stares at the pictures and wonders for the first time in a very long while who his parents were and why they just left him at the hospital unclaimed. Who does that? Sebastian wonders how different his life would have been had he had two loving parents, or even loving grandparents. Would he still have wound up here as a slave? Would he have had a different life? Would he have ever met Kindle or gone off to University as he had planned to do before making a mess of his life? Sebastian quietly snaps the compact closed and returns it to his pocket. He walks over to the mini bar and pours himself another glass of scotch. Sebastian gulps it down and quietly lets himself out of Hunter Ryan's suite. He walks downstairs and lets himself out through the servant's door. Sebastian walks across the grounds and enters the servant's quarters. He wonders if Francois is awake. He stops at Francois' door and presses his ear against the door. There is no sound coming from the other side of the door. Sebastian isn't sure if Francois is even in the room. He could still be with a client. Sebastian decides not to knock on the door, sleep is a precious commodity in this life. He wouldn't want to wake Francois or his bunkmates if they were sleeping. Sebastian walks to his small room and climbs into bed. He looks around the small room. Sergei's asleep in his bed, Emmett's in the shower. Sebastian closes his eyes and allows the scotch to do its magic. Sebastian falls into a deep scotch induced sleep before Emmett shuts off the water in the shower.

Five hours later the alarm clock rings. Sebastian gets up and showers. Emmett's up and dressed in the chauffeur clothing that Sebastian used to wear. Sergei is allowed to sleep for another hour before breakfast. Sergei opens his eyes and mumbles something incoherently. Sergei rolls over and faces the wall, he goes back to sleep. Sebastian pulls the compact out of the pocket of his robes and places it in his jeans pocket. He quietly leaves the room and walks down the hall towards the dining hall. Upon entering the kitchen, he looks around for Francois. Francois is in the back of the kitchen mixing powdered milk for cereal. He walks over to Francois, "morning." Francois nervously looks up as Sebastian approaches, gives him a friendly nod and returns his attention to the powdered milk mixture.

Sebastian reaches into his pocket, wraps his hand around the cool metal compact and pulls it out of his pocket. Sebastian looks around, no one pays any attention to Francois or Sebastian. It's almost as if they're invisible to everyone else around them. He reaches his hand out towards Francois. Francois stares nervously at him, stretches his hand out towards Sebastian and accepts the compact. Francois stares at the compact, "how did you get this?"

"Luc," Sebastian answers.

Francois stares at Sebastian, "Merci."

"Votre accueil" Sebastian says as he turns to leave.

"Sebastian?" Francois whispers. Sebastian turns back towards Francois. Francois pulls a plate out from underneath the counter and removes the cheese cloth wrapped around it. On the plate is a chocolate éclair. "When I picked up the food order this morning, the head chef Antonio gave me this. Told me he only had one left this morning, gave it to me to eat. I was saving it till after I washed all the dishes, you know when I'm all alone. Kind of a reward so to speak." Francois pulls out a knife and cuts the éclair in half, he hands half to Sebastian. They walk to the back door together and silently watch the sunrise together enjoying their private treat. "Merci, Francois, can I ask are they your parents and grandparents?"

"Oui, mon pere's parents. The police gave me ma mere's compact and mon pere's wallet after the accident. I took the pictures from mon pere's wallet and placed them in ma mere's compact. It's all I have of my parents and grandparents. I never knew ma mere's parents. They died shortly after I was born. Mon pere's parents also died when I was young. I have a few faint memories of them." Francois tells Sebastian.

"Your father's parents are Monsieur Corbett's parents? Yes?" Sebastian asks.

"Oui."

"Francois, was Monsieur Corbett married?"

"Non."

"Who is Luc's mother then?" Sebastian nervously asks.

Francois nervously glances around making sure no one can overhear them before deciding they are alone and it's safe to tell. "A former servant named Odessa from the Ukraine. Uncle Luscious never speaks of her. Luc is a bastard child with Corbett blood. Luc was conceived and born out of wedlock. As far as he knows, his mother died shortly after childbirth. She just disappeared, more than likely her contract was sold. Uncle Luscious kept her son. Gave him the Corbett name and raised him as a single child." Francois answers.

Francois and Sebastian watch the sun rise, they return to the kitchen and serve breakfast. Sebastian cleans up the dining area while Francois washes the dishes. They are the last two to finish and leave the kitchen. They head out to the stables to feed, groom, and exercise the horses. Sebastian begins to realize that he no longer feels any anger or hatred towards Francois. He finds they both have had their share of pain and that they have more in common with one another than he had ever allowed himself to think about or admit.

Chapter 20

Sergei's illness hits in the middle of November. Sebastian notices Sergei's discomfort and trouble breathing over dinner. Sebastian and Emmett support Sergei's weight as they assist him back down the hall to their small room. Sebastian leaves Emmett at Sergei's bedside and heads up to Monsieur Corbett's office. Sebastian knocks on the office door. Luc opens the door. Sebastian requests permission to enter the office, Luc allows him to enter. He walks to the center of the office and stands at attention his hands at his sides.

"Sebastian, what brings you to my office?" Luscious Corbett asks.

"Monsieur, it's my roommate Sergei. He is ill. He cannot breathe, he is burning up. Sergei needs the doc. Please. You must help him."

Luscious Corbett picks up the phone and calls the doctors clinic. A little over an hour later Dr. Maboob arrives at the Chalet. Sergei's fever spikes above one hundred and two degrees. Forty-five minutes later Sergei slips into the endless sleep. Dr. Maboob fights for two days to keep Sergei alive. On the third morning Sergei gasps his last breath and peacefully passes away.

Dr Maboob informs Sebastian and Emmet that Sergei's death was caused by a rare strain of Meningitis. He will need to test both Sebastian and Emmett for any signs of the same rare strain. Emmett and Sebastian are quarantined for four days before being told they are healthy and not infected with the Meningitis virus.

Sebastian, Francois, and Emmett bury Sergei's body at the edge of the woods behind the stables. Sebastian kneels next to Sergei's grave, lays wildflowers on his grave and recites Robert Frost's poem Nothing Gold Can Stay.

Sebastian punches the ground, screams at the heavens, and openly cries. He doesn't care what Emmett or Francois thinks of him. Sergei was his friend, his brother, the first to befriend him, the first to give him any trust, and most importantly the first to earn Sebastian's trust. It takes 20 minutes to calm Sebastian down and an additional 10 minutes to get him to agree to leave Sergei's grave side. Sebastian marks the tree next to Sergei's grave, so he'll always be able to locate it.

This is the fate they will all face one day. Their bodies will be wrapped in a plain white sheet, a six-foot grave will be dug, and they will be placed in the cold, damp ground. Hopefully someone will mourn for them and give them some kind of graveside service. There will be no record of the death. They're memories only kept alive by the memories of the living, the memories of one another. Sergei's memory kept alive by those closest to him. It's a cruel fate, but a fate they will all inevitably face one day.

Sebastian returns to Sergei's grave almost daily and for the first time ever, Luscious Corbett allows one of his servants to mourn the loss of a fellow servant. Sebastian is granted time to mourn Sergei's loss before returning to chauffeur status. Each morning a GPS monitor is placed on Sebastian's left wrist. Luscious opens his top desk drawer and pulls out a whip or paddle. He lies it out on his desk as a cruel reminder of what Sebastian can expect should Sebastian wreck the new Bentley or attempt to rabbit. Sebastian drives the guests and clients around Paris, to and from the train station and airport. He picks up and delivers packages all over Paris. He never asks about the contents, he finds he no longer cares about the packages or its contents.

Sebastian falls into a deep depression. Emmett keeps an eye on him, worried that he will do something crazy or stupid and get himself killed if left to his own devices. Sergei's death affects Sebastian in new ways. It opens up a new dark place in his mind that allows him to ignore all fear and pain. He lets go of the humiliation and faces the endless brutality with a new dominant wisdom. He no longer needs alcohol to perform his duties. He is no longer the defenseless submissive creature he once was. He faces the cameras with a new defiance. He fights what he can and accepts what he cannot. He no longer feels anything except the empty hollow numbness that was once his heart.

My Dearest Kindle,

I have lost someone close to me, someone I held with great esteem. I have come to realize that we all face the same uncertain end. I can't imagine my life ending out of my control. Unrecorded and only kept alive by the memories of those chosen to remember me.

I have to find a way to make sure that when the time comes, I go out by my choice, my way. I can't let all this have been for nothing. I will fight till there is nothing left to fight for until my last dying breath...

Kindle, be a better stronger person than I, make your life worth living, and make sure it means something important. Do amazing things with your life; change how people look at the world. Change how they view their way of living. You're going to be an amazing interior designer, hopefully one day I'll get to be the architect I always dreamed of becoming. Changing the world one building at a time.

Much Love
Sebastian

Chapter 21

CHRISTIAN RAINES ARRIVES EARLY AT THE AIRPORT. Kindle's flying home for the winter holidays. Christian hasn't seen his daughter since the end of the summer solstice. He and his wife Jenna are excited to have their daughter returning home for the holidays. Jenna Raines hasn't stopped shopping or baking since finding out that Kindle was coming home. Christian will soon be broke from all of Jenna's shopping and plans. He loves his wife dearly but soon he will have to put his foot down and put an end to all her shopping and all her extravagant plans.

Kindle Raines walks down the corridor, spots her father waiting for her out in the concourse. Kindles face lights up, she stretches her arms out and warmly embraces her father. She feels like a child returning home from a long summer vacation to her family's loving embrace.

Kindle talks her father's ear off all the way to the baggage claim. She has so many things to tell him about the big American city, and all about her studies at NYU.

Christian Raines loves his daughter. Her chatter reminds him of Jenna when she gets an exciting idea stuck in her head and can't let it go, till she has told him every last detail. Kindle resembles her mother with her beautiful long, dark hair and a slim figure. She has her father's green eyes and his kind, warm smile. His daughter keeps up her constant excited chatter all the way to the car. Kindle has brought home part of her portfolio she's working on in her interior design classes back in the states. She can't wait to share it with her parents and show them how much she has learned from her professors and studies.

"I forgot how beautiful the French countryside is. Sometimes I miss the beauty and simplicity of home. The city is always so vibrant and alive."

"Do you regret choosing to go to school in the states so far from home in such a big city?"

"Never, papa, just sometimes I wish I was a little closer to home. The city is exciting, always so full of life and vibrant colors. It can just be a bit overwhelming at times."

"Don't tell your mother that, she'll want you to move back home immediately." Christian laughs and teases his daughter.

The squad car pulls up to the house. Jenna Raines is watching from the kitchen window for Christian and Kindle to arrive home. From the kitchen's back door, Jenna bursts out to greet her daughter and husband. Kindle excitedly climbs out of the car and embraces her mother. "Welcome home Kindle, it's so good to have you home. How was your flight?" Jenna Raines asks.

"Long and tiring, I'm glad to be home." Kindle walks arm in arm with her mother into the house. Christian Raines laughs and shakes his head, how quickly he's been forgotten. He grabs Kindle's luggage out of the back of the car and carries it into the house enjoying the sound of his wife and daughter carrying on in the kitchen. For the first time in a long time, Christian realizes just how quiet their small country house is when his daughters away at school.

The house is a simple county farm but smells like a restaurant and bakery. Jenna has been cooking all Kindle's favorite foods in anticipation of her arrival. Jenna stripped and washed all Kindles bedding before remaking her bed. She spent the day vacuuming and dusting. Christian follows his daughter up the stairs and down the hallway towards her bedroom. He deposits her luggage on the bed and smiles at his daughter. Christian kisses his daughter on the top of her head and turns to leave the room.

"Papa? Any news?" Kindle softly asks. He smiles sadly at his daughter. He hates the answer he must give. "Honey, I'm sorry, no new leads." Christian embraces his daughter. He pulls away from his daughter, smiles sadly at her and leaves her standing next to her bed, she will need privacy to unpack her belongings before joining them in the kitchen for supper.

Kindle slowly unpacks. Sets up the few pictures she has of her and Sebastian from school and visits to the farmhouse on her bed side table and drafting desk. Her heart aches for her missing fiancé. The smell of eggplant parmigiana and garlic knots catch Kindle's attention. She picks up her portfolio lying on the foot of the bed and heads downstairs to join her parents in the kitchen for supper. Kindle is excited to be home, and anxious to enjoy her mother's home cooking. The time and love her mother puts into her cooking makes the food extra delicious.

Kindle joins her parents in the sitting room after helping both her parents clear the table and wash the dishes. She lays out her portfolio. Excitedly shows her parents all her new ideas. Kindle shows them her plans to turn a small living space into a comfortable environment. New and exciting kitchen and bath ideas. How to take old antiques, clean them up and turn them into new and exciting pieces. Kindle will start her toughest courses after the winter break so she has been busy drafting and drawing all her designs. Jenna and Christian Raines are impressed with all of Kindles ideas and hard work.

Chapter 22

SEBASTIAN LIES AWAKE IN HIS BED, STARING AT THE ALARM clock. 0248. The winter holidays have arrived, and nothing has changed. Kindle will be home celebrating Christmas with her family. Sebastian will be offered to private lonely clients who have no one else to spend the holiday season with. Sebastian stares at Sergei's empty bunk. Emmett moans in his sleep. Emmett's blanket falls off the bed and lands on the floor. Sebastian gets up and picks the blanket up off the floor and covers Emmett's shivering body. He lies back down in his bed and stares again at the clock 0255. Unable to sleep Sebastian gets up and paces the hallway. It's on his third round that he notices Francois sitting up in the commons room. Sebastian walks over to the corner where Francois is sitting alone. "Trouble sleeping?" Sebastian whispers.

"Yeah, you as well? I heard you pacing the hallway." Francois whispers back.

"Yeah; do you ever feel like there's a whole world out there passing you by with no clue that you even exist? We are to be barely seen, and never heard. We are to pleasure but are treated as if we are no more than a nuisance." Sebastian angrily whispers.

"Sebastian you're the strongest one of us all, is something bothering you?"

"Tomorrow morning all of France will celebrate Christmas. Kindle will wake up and celebrate Noel with her family. I'll wake up in the same bed I've woken up in for the past two and a half years. I'll scrape by another day as a servant to the rich and lonely. Kindle will attend church services, open gifts, and eat food that is home cooked and do all this with her family. My family here will spend the day serving as slaves. As far as I can tell, the only way out is death. No one ever pays their contract off. I'll never see her again, never hold her again. I'll never hear her soft melodic voice again. I'll never gaze into her sapphire green eyes or run my hands through her soft dark brown hair. She always smells like vanilla. It was subtle, but always on the breeze." Sebastian mournfully whispers.

"It's the holidays, man, makes you more sentimental. Makes us all more depressed, or crazy. Take your pick. This time of year is always the hardest for me. It's when I miss my parents the most. The holidays were when our entire family got together. Luc would come and stay with my family for the holidays. Luc's father always joined us on the eve of Noel, but Luc, he would come and stay at our house for 10 days." Francois almost smiles as he pictures the memory.

"The sisters at the orphanage raised money each year to buy each child at the orphanage two small gifts for Christmas. Before coming to live at the Chalet and serve Monsieur Corbett, I spent Noel with Kindle's family. Her mother cooked the entire meal from scratch. Her mom is an amazing cook." Sebastian sadly whispers.

"Francois, why are you up, what's wrong?"

"My small room has suddenly become too large and too empty."

"What do you mean? What's happened to Edgar and Victor?"

"They're contracts were sold, they left earlier today while the rest of us were working in the stables and kitchens. I didn't even get to tell them goodbye."

"Francois, I'm sorry. I didn't know. It's Noel and you're all alone. We have an empty bed in our room. Why don't you move in with Emmett and me? It hasn't been the same since Sergei passed away."

"You'd be OK with that? Emmett would be OK with that? You'd trust me and allow me to move in with you and Emmett?"

"I told you, the past is the past. I've learned to let go of the past. You have worked hard, and you have proven that you're now one of us. Emmet will enjoy having someone to talk to when I'm not around. Emmett's still young; he needs guidance and companionship."

"Merci, I'll pack up and move in tomorrow."

"I'll tell Jurai that you'll be moving into our room, which will give Jurai an empty room to place the new recruits. Speaking of new recruits, why are they getting younger and younger? Have you noticed how young the newest servants are?"

"Younger offerings make more money, younger recruits can work harder, longer hours. Longer contracts mean more money. The younger ones make Corbett more money.

"There are some sick people out there that don't care about age. There was a time when Corbett wouldn't have bought or sold anyone under the age of 16, now most are as young as 11 or 12."

"I thought I was going crazy, I noticed that the help was getting younger. I thought I was just getting old." Sebastian tells Francois, they both laugh.

"Thought I was the only one feeling like I was getting older and everyone else was getting younger. I think it's why Corbett sold Victor and Edgar; they weren't making a lot of money any longer as personal offerings. They didn't look young enough anymore. Why is it that some of us age faster than others? You still look as young as the first day you walked through the Chalet's doors two and a half years ago."

"Some handle the stress better than others. Most rely heavily on drugs and alcohol to deal with what is expected of them. Others have a secret place they are able to escape to within their minds, less stress when you can just go someplace else. I escape to the Louvre or to the Opera. By escaping it's a lot less stressful. Two years ago, I thought a lot about suicide. Now I just escape and afterward scrub almost all the skin off my body in the shower. It's not healthy or right but it helps me to deal with it."

"I haven't found that place yet."

"I'm sorry to hear that Francois, you have to dig deep within yourself and find that safe happy place. It will save your life."

Francois thinks about Sebastian's advice. Sebastian and Francois sit in silence.

"I guess I should get to bed. Sunrise is around the corner, Joyeux Noel, Francois."

"Joyeux Noel, Sebastian."

Francois walks back to his empty room, packs his few belongings, and places them in a small box. He places the small box on his nightstand and lies down in bed. Sebastian walks back to his small room, picks Emmett's blanket back up off the floor and tucks it firmly around Emmett's thin body. Sebastian writes a letter to Jurai informing him that Francois will be moving out of his small room and bunking with him and Emmett, therefore, allowing the new recruits to move out of the hayloft in the stables and into Francois' old room. He walks back out into the hallway and places the letter in Jurai's letter box. He returns to the small room, and checks on Emmett one last time before turning the light off. He lies in bed and closes his eyes.

Two hours later, the alarm clock rings. Sebastian and Emmett shower, clean up, and report to the kitchen to prepare and serve breakfast. Sebastian tells Emmett that Francois will be moving in with them to make room for the new young recruits that are currently sleeping in the hay loft above the horse's stables.

Jurai signs off on Francois moving in with Emmett and Sebastian. Francois quickly moves in after breakfast. Sebastian and Emmett wash dishes and clean the kitchen, in the late morning the servants line up in the main dining area wearing red and green robes. They sing carols for the guests. The rest of the holiday is spent working. For four young men sleeping in the horse's stables, Noel is the celebration of getting a new warm room to sleep in with beds and working electricity. For a few there is something to celebrate. For the captives, it's just another day as a slave working laundry or in the kitchens. Another day in a life of hell. There's no redemption, not even during the holiday. Sebastian spends the day on his knees. When he isn't pleasing enough or quick enough, he is whipped with leather, others are beaten with a wooden paddle with holes drilled into it. Beaten and bruised Sebastian's day ends with a GPS monitor and a long uncomfortable trip to the train station. Francois spends Noel begging for the pain to stop, begging for one last chance to prove he can do better. Emmett spends the holiday pleasuring complete strangers on his hands and knees collared and leashed like a dog.

"Pornography" and "adult entertainment" are words used all too often to cover up Human Trafficking.

- A 21 CAMPAIGN

There are 20.9 million victims of human trafficking globally.

— Human Trafficking Advocacy News

Modern day slavery is occurring in the vast supply chains that fuel our global economy, causing human tragedy and damaging some of the world's most trusted brands.

— Amy Sobel
Vice President, Anti Human Trafficking Campaign

An estimated 21 million victims are entrapped by this practice, and the number is growing at about 800,000 per year.

— Dr. Bob Eccles

Chapter 23

JURAI INSTRUCTS SEBASTIAN THAT MONSIEUR CORBETT IS looking for him. He instructs him to shower, dress, and report to the branding stall in the back of the stables. Sebastian's hand instinctively reaches for his left shoulder. He can still feel the brand through the thin fabric of his shirt. A letter C forever burned into his skin. The brand is something Sebastian has learned to ignore and most days, he barely notices it. He's learned to ignore the painful truth behind his servitude. But now he is reminded of the excruciating burning sensation he'd felt that day three years ago after he had been branded as Monsieur Corbett's property. The pain and humiliation he had felt for several days and weeks after losing his freedom and basically his human rights. Sebastian groans as he crawls out of bed and walks to the bathroom. He showers as fast as possible. You don't keep Monsieur Corbett waiting any longer than necessary when ordered to present one's self to him. Sebastian puts on a clean pair of work clothes. Brushes his teeth, combs his hair and leaves his small room. He walks past the dining hall, considers stopping in and grabbing a small amount of food to carry with him but decides against it. He reminds himself you don't keep Monsieur Corbett waiting. Sebastian turns and walks away from the dining hall. He walks towards the end of the hallway, his mind racing. Sebastian thinks of the past three years and what he has learned about whom he is and what he is capable of overcoming. Sebastian opens the door and walks out into the warm spring air. While Sebastian's servitude at Monsieur Corbett's Chalet has been the worst three years of his life; Sebastian realizes that the pain and humiliation has taught him things about himself that he had either denied himself in the past or had simply just not known.

First, Sebastian has learned that the last three years of his life have been full of the worst kind of misery imaginable. Sebastian's inner strengths have made him stronger than he ever thought possible. His inner strengths have protected him and taught him how to live through the worst kinds of beatings and rapes that would kill most ordinary people. He has learned how to remove himself from the worst sexual assaults and experiences that anyone should ever be forced to endure, much less have to live through in their day-to-day lives.

Second, Sebastian has learned that forgiveness is the key to survival. Forgiving the worst imaginable crime and letting go of the past. His alliance with Francois had taught him that.

Third and most importantly Sebastian no longer needed all the answers to his past. He was learning who he was, what made him the man that he was becoming and that was enough.

Fourth, while Monsieur Luscious Corbett physically owned him, his identity was what he made of it. His values. His beliefs. They couldn't take his core values away from him. No matter how hard they tried.

Fifth, last but certainly not least: if all else failed, it was Kindle's loving memory that would help him endure and would keep him alive. Give him a fighting chance at survival.

Sebastian stops walking. He's just outside the stables. The smell of burning flesh hangs on the morning air. Sebastian's hand instinctively reaches for his left shoulder. He can feel the impression of the brand through the thin fabric of his shirt. The gut wrenching sounds of screaming and grunting reminds Sebastian of the pain and misery one endures when being branded. It was the first horror that he had lived through three years ago. It was the first realization that his life was no longer his own. That he'd sold his soul to the devil.

Sebastian opens the stable door and steps into the branding stall. He stops dead in his tracks. Tomas's young and all too familiar face stares back at him. A ghost from Sebastian's past. Tomas lived at the same orphanage as Sebastian. The all too familiar brand burnt into Tomas' left shoulder.

Sebastian's stomach twists into a painful knot. Nausea washes over him. Uncontrollably, he turns and grabs the nearest wooden bucket, steps back out of the branding stall and hurls into the bucket. Shaking, barely able to stand Sebastian cleans himself up as fast as possible. Quickly composes himself and returns to the branding stall. Luscious Corbett glares at Sebastian, his moment of weakness will cost him dearly.

Tomas stares at Sebastian. Recognition flickers across Tomas' face. Sebastian prays to the God he no longer believes in that Tomas will be smart enough to keep silent. Sebastian turns back towards Monsieur Corbett and awaits his instructions. Luscious studies Sebastian's face. Disapproval etched deeply into his expression.

"Retirez votre chemise!" Luscious growls.

Hands shaking, the painful knot returning to Sebastian's stomach, Sebastian takes a deep calming breath and unbuttons his flannel shirt. Sebastian looks nervously at Corbett and removes his shirt, laying it across the nearest railing. Shaking from head to toe, controlling his breathing, and holding down the urge to vomit again Sebastian lifts his eyes. He stares at the red-hot branding iron. He looks up and meets Corbett's eyes.

"Tempting, very tempting Sebastian. No not today. You're here for a very different purpose." Luscious sneers at Sebastian.

Sebastian turns to face Tomas. Tomas stares wide eyed at Sebastian's left shoulder, realization sinking in.

Sebastian turns back to Corbett. "Monsieur, how may I serve you?"

Luscious Corbett turns his attention back towards the red-hot branding iron sitting in the flames. "Sebastian have you ever branded anyone?" Luscious asks.

"Non, Monsieur." Sebastian nervously answers as he again eyes the red-hot branding iron.

Luscious walks over and picks the branding iron up by its leather handle, then motions for Sebastian to take the hot branding iron from his grasp. Fear consumes Sebastian as his shaking right hand reaches for the branding iron. Sebastian grasps the leather handle and takes it from Luscious Corbett's strong grasp. Sebastian's grasp tightens as the weight of the branding iron consumes him. The heat radiates off the branding iron. It would be the worst kind of misery imaginable if Sebastian dropped the branding iron, a punishment he had no intention or desire to inflict upon himself.

Sebastian looks to his master for instructions, Luscious smiles in an evil kind of way at Sebastian. "You fear it, do you not?" Luscious Corbett asks, studying Sebastian's face.

"Oui, Monsieur," his shaking voice answers. There is no point in lying. Luscious Corbett can read the fear etched into Sebastian's eyes and face.

"Always truthful." Luscious sneers.

Luscious Corbett grasps the branding irons leather handle and removes it from Sebastian's shaking grasp. He studies Sebastian's face one last time, registers the fear in his eyes. Luscious tosses the branding iron into a nearby metal bucket filled with water. The water in the bucket immediately begins to boil as scalding hot steam rolls of the branding iron and into the air. Sebastian takes a deep breath and shakily releases it.

"Fear is control. Fear is what keeps you alive." Luscious Corbett instructs Tomas.

Tomas stares at Sebastian, turns his head and nods his understanding to Corbett. Luscious hands Sebastian his flannel shirt. Sebastian accepts the shirt but waits for permission to put it back on. Luscious walks in a slow circle around Sebastian. Running his hands over Sebastian's scars on his back and shoulders. Luscious finally instructs Sebastian to put his shirt back on. Sebastian puts his flannel shirt back on and slowly buttons it with shaking hands.

"You may feed the horses and muck out the stalls." Luscious instructs Sebastian.

Sebastian takes one last look at Tomas, pain etched across his young, handsome facial features, his body slumped forward. Sebastian watches as the needle enters Tomas' arm, watches as Luscious pushes the plunger that feeds the heroin into Tomas' system. Sebastian backs out of the stall, turns, and runs to the far side of the stables. His need to escape overwhelms him. He finds a restless kind of energy feeding and caring for Corbett's prize-winning racehorses.

Sebastian tries to erase the image of Corbett's red-hot branding iron from his mind and tries to settle in and find a rhythm to his work. Unable to find his usual peace caring for the horses, Sebastian's mind races in circles. The putrid smell of burning flesh haunts his memory. Sebastian realizes that Corbett's knowledge of his fear is a weapon that will be used against him in the future. Sebastian grooms and feeds the horses. His usual energy sapped out of him. Painful memories replacing it.

Sebastian spends the day in the stables mucking out the stalls, organizing anything and everything to keep Monsieur Corbett happy and to distract himself from thinking about the red-hot branding iron sitting in a bucket of boiling water and steam just on the other side of the stables. As the sun sets, Sebastian realizes he has no desire to eat or drink anything. Instead, he heads straight to the shower and lets the water drown out his fears and sorrows. The water falls off his body and pounds against the cement floor. He stares down at his once muscular tanned body and realizes just how thin and pale he has become over the past three years at the Chalet.

Sebastian turns the water off, grabs a towel and presses it tightly against his face to muffle the sounds of his screams. He dries himself off, composes himself, and dresses in his dark navy-blue robes. Sebastian walks by the dining hall and looks in there is no sign of Tomas. Francois and Emmett are sitting together towards the back of the hall. Sebastian notices again just how young most of the new faces are. He again wonders how much longer till Luscious Corbett loses interest in him and what that means for his future. The thought terrifies him, panic rises and his heart pounds like a sledgehammer against his ribs. Sebastian turns and walks down the hall; he heads out the door across the field towards Monsieur Corbett's office.

Sebastian knocks on Corbett's office door and waits.

"Enterer."

Sebastian nervously turns the knob, opens the door, and enters the office. Tomas is on his knees next to Corbett's desk. He is dressed in a red short sleeved shirt and a pair of cutoff jean shorts. He has socks but no shoes on his feet. Sebastian closes the door and walks to the middle of the office. Standing straight with his arms down by his sides. Sebastian awaits his orders. Ignoring Tomas' pleading eyes, he looks to Corbett for instructions. Luscious eyes Sebastian suspiciously studying his facial features.

"You know one another. Your eyes and face tell me it's more than just a casual acquaintance?" Luscious Corbett asks.

"Oui, Monsieur."

Corbett stares at Sebastian expecting more information.

"We are from the same past so to speak. We grew up at the same orphanage."

"Good, then you won't mind caring for him and making sure he lives through the next few days. If Tomas lives, he'll start his training and begin working," Luscious Corbett instructs Sebastian.

Luscious motions for Sebastian to assist Tomas to his feet. Sebastian walks to Tomas' side, roughly pulls Tomas to his feet. He looks to Corbett for permission to leave the office.

"Any screw ups, and the branding iron will await you, understood?" Luscious asks.

"Oui, Monsieur" Sebastian nervously answers.

"Votre rejete," Luscious instructs Sebastian.

Sebastian turns and half carries Tomas across the room and out the side entrance into the kitchen, he walks him through the kitchen and out the back door towards the servant's quarters.

Sebastian notices Francois walking ahead of him.

"Francois, wait up s'lil vous plait."

Francois turns, "who is this?" His curiosity peaked.

"Tomas" Sebastian grunts in response. "I'm in need of liquor. Can you get me some, s'il vous plait? Without getting caught?" Sebastian inquires of Francois.

"Oui, how much do you need?"

"Enough liquor to keep him silent and to help him feel no pain for the next few days."

"I know exactly what you need. Give me 10 minutes." Francois smiles and turns towards the main guest house. Sebastian escorts Tomas to his room in the servants quarters. He sits Tomas on his bed and awaits Francois' return. Ten minutes later Francois returns with a bottle of whiskey and a bottle of scotch from the guest house pub. Sebastian opens the scotch and instructs Tomas to drink the entire bottle. Tomas takes three long gulps before passing out from a mixture of heroin and scotch. Sebastian and Francois loosen his clothing and tuck him into Sebastian's bed.

"Sleep in my bed tonight, Monsieur Corbett will be taking Emmett and I into Paris tonight to service clientele on Embassy Row. We won't return till morning." Francois explains to Sebastian.

"Merci, Francois, you are kind."

Sebastian checks on Tomas to make sure he is still breathing and turns the lights off. He walks to the dining hall and accepts some fruit and crackers from Emmett who is finishing his cleaning shift in the kitchen. "Merci, Emmett." Sebastian finally feels hunger. "Thought you might be hungry, haven't seen you at any of today's meals." Emmett answers.

You may choose to look the other way, but you can never again say that you did not know.

- William Wilberforce

Every 30 seconds another person becomes a slave.

— A21 Campaign

There are more slaves today than ever before in history.

— A21 Campaign

Less than 1% of slaves are ever rescued.

— A21 Campaign

Chapter 24

SEBASTIAN WAKES UP. TOMAS IS MOANING. THE HEROIN AND liquor have worn off. Sebastian looks at the clock. 0200. Sebastian sits up in Francois' bed and collects his bearings. He gets out of bed and walks the few feet to the other side of the small room. He sits on the bed next to Tomas. Sebastian grabs the half empty bottle of scotch from underneath the bed and puts the bottle to Tomas' mouth instructing him to drink. Tomas opens his mouth. Sebastian pours the remaining scotch down his throat. Tomas stares at Sebastian. "It's OK, we'll talk in the morning when the sun's replaced the moon, for now, sleep. Votre coffre-fort."

It tastes like a lie to tell him he is safe. What else can he say? Tomas is safer with Sebastian at least for now. He sits on the edge of Tomas' bed and watches Tomas restlessly toss and turn in his sleep. He feels empathy for Tomas. He remembers the all consuming pain and burning sensation left by the fire-hot branding iron. Sebastian waits for the scotch to take its full effect. After 10 minutes, Tomas begins to calm down. He lies still and breathes heavily. Sebastian presses his fingers against the side of Tomas' neck. Tomas' pulse is fast but steady and strong. Sebastian watches Tomas sleep. He stands up, bends over, and tucks the blanket tightly around Tomas' body. Sebastian quietly pads back across the room and climbs back into Francois bed. He prays that the rest of Tomas' night is spent peacefully sleeping. Sebastian rolls over and faces the wall. He stretches out in the bed and closes his eyes. Sleep comes quickly. No nightmares, just hours of dreamless sleep.

Morning comes all too quickly. Emmett and Francois' return awakens Sebastian. Sebastian sits up and blinks his eyes. He looks towards his bed for Tomas.

"He's already up, heard him in the shower." Francois tells Sebastian.

Sebastian gets up and stretches, walks the few feet across the room and knocks on the bathroom door. There is no answer, only silence on the other side of the door. He turns the knob slowly and opens the door, pokes his head around the door frame. Tomas is sitting in the back corner of the shower stall, his knees pulled up tightly against his chest, his arms wrapped tightly around his legs as if willing himself not to fall over. Water cascades over his small, naked body. Tomas' head is down he's crying quietly into his arms. A sharp pain clutches at Sebastian's heart as he intrudes upon Tomas' private moment of pain and misery.

Sebastian steps into the bathroom and closes the door. Tomas doesn't move. Sebastian turns the water off and grabs a clean dry towel off the rack. He crouches against the rear shower wall and lowers his body next to Tomas'. He wraps a towel around his naked, shaking body. He rubs Tomas' shoulders and back.

"It's OK we're all a bit scared at first. The first few days here are hell. Monsieur Corbett just wants to remind you that your life is no longer yours to control, prove who's really in charge and that we are to do as we are told. No exceptions, no questions asked. You're not alone in this. We all have been through it. Francois, Emmett, and I will help you as best we can. We are your brothers." Sebastian informs Tomas.

Tomas leans against Sebastian and sobs into his shoulder his body shaking violently. Sebastian patiently waits for Tomas to calm down, for his body to stop shaking.

A soft knock on the bathroom door draws Sebastian's attention. Francois opens the door and pokes his head around the door. "Emmett has some clean clothes that might fit Tomas." Francois hands a clean pair of shorts, a clean shirt, and a new pair of black briefs around the door.

Sebastian leans his weight into the wall and pushes up against the wall till he is standing. He walks over to the door and accepts the clothing from Francois. "Merci, Francois. Tell Emmett, Merci." Francois closes the door behind him to give Tomas privacy to get dressed. Sebastian turns and heads back to Tomas' side. Hands shaking Tomas reaches for the clean clothing. Sebastian turns his back, allowing Tomas some privacy to get dressed. Feeling warmer and better, Tomas follows Sebastian out of the bathroom and across the small room to Sebastian's makeshift nightstand. Sebastian hands Tomas a hairbrush, toothpaste, a toothbrush, and deodorant. After Tomas is finished cleaning up Sebastian instructs Tomas to sit on the bed and wait while he walks down the hallway to the dining hall to see what he can get for him and Tomas to eat. Sebastian picks out some stale pastries, some cut up apples, biscuits, cold ham, and eggs. There is no milk or juice this morning, so he grabs two cups for water. Sebastian leaves the dining hall and returns to the small room that he now shares with Tomas, Emmett, and Francois. Tomas eats both plates of food, leaving only the cut-up apples for Sebastian to eat. Sebastian watches in fascination as Tomas eats. "Tomas, when was the last time you had anything to eat?" Sebastian asks.

"Three days ago, before I arrived here." Tomas answers.

"You've been here for three days? Where have you been? Why have none of us seen you before yesterday?" Francois asks.

Francois, Emmet, and Sebastian exchange concerned glances. What had happened before Sebastian had seen him in the branding stall in the stables yesterday.

"Until yesterday, I was locked in a small room just off the kitchens in the main guest house. I could smell the food, hear the kitchen staff. I wasn't given anything to eat or drink for three days." Tomas answers as he gulps down his second glass of water.

Sebastian passes Tomas a glass of milk made with a packet of powdered milk from his nightstand. "It's powdered milk but it's better than the water from the tap," Sebastian explains.

Tomas swallows the milk down and smiles at Sebastian for the first time since being reunited. "Reminds me of the milk rations at the orphanage during the lean winter months." Tomas grins.

"Yeah, the winter months were leaner than the summer months." Sebastian laughs.

"Tomas, what happened to you? How did you end up here?" Sebastian asks.

"After graduating, I left the orphanage. I thought I could do better out on my own. I made some bad choices in who I trusted. I got mixed up with the wrong kind of people. I ended up homeless and alone on the streets. I was too proud to go back to the orphanage and ask for help. I needed money, so I started turning tricks on the streets of Paris. I became a street hustler. Did whatever it took to get money. That's how I met Luc. He offered me a job at his father's Chalet. It sounded so much better than just working and living off the streets. We arrived here at the Chalet well after 0200. Luc offered me a drink and introduced me to his father Monsieur Corbett. One drink turned into something like three or four I don't remember, I think I lost count. I woke up restrained in a small room just off the main dining room kitchens. I could hear the kitchen staff. I banged on the door and called out for help, but no one would answer my calls. After two days, Luc returned. He opened the door and dragged me out of the small room and across the kitchen to Monsieur Corbett's office. He put a gun to my head and fired. I remember putting my arms in front of my face and crying out. Luc just laughed at me. There were no bullets in the gun. I was forced out to the stables and restrained to a chair, I was punched and kicked repeatedly. Luc again aimed the gun at my head and told me to beg for my life. I stared at him and begged him to kill me instead. Luc loaded the gun and pointed it at my chest and fired three times. I pissed myself. Turns out all three were blanks. My heart pounding, I cried and begged for mercy. Luc just smiled that evil smile," Tomas explains.

"That's when they branded you?" Sebastian asks.

"Oui," Tomas answers. "Then you arrived. I recognized you immediately. I thought you were one of Corbett's men till he had you remove your shirt. I saw the same matching brand on your shoulder. I understood than that you are just as much a prisoner as I am. After that there was just fear."

"Tomas, I'm sorry. I wish I could tell you that life here at the Chalet is a happy one but that would taste a lie. There are very few good days. Most are hard and exhausting. Some are pure misery. Monsieur Corbett was right about one thing. Fear's what keeps most of us alive. When you stop fearing the pain, when you stop caring about your life, when all your fears are gone and he no longer has a hold over you, that's when it's over, that's when death welcomes you as a friend," Sebastian fearfully explains.

Sebastian stares at Tomas, opens his mouth and closes it, clears his throat and tries again.

"Tomas, have you seen Kindle? Is she alright? Did she go to NYU as planned?" Sebastian asks.

Tomas smiles sadly at Sebastian. "That's what has kept you alive all this time.

Kindle's memory? I wondered how you survived here for so long. Do you know you have been missing for three years? Have you been here the entire time?"

"Oui, three years." Sebastian answers.

"Kindles hair is longer, she is thinner. Your disappearance hit her hard. She comes home from New York every holiday. Kindle and her family still volunteer at the orphanage every holiday. She and her father have never stopped searching all of France for you.

Sadly, I'm afraid they are no closer to finding you. The Paris Police have no leads and no idea about Monsieur Corbett's business here at the Chalet."

Sebastian digests Tomas's news. It pains him to think of Kindle so frail and in so much pain over his disappearance.

"We will be working in the field today. It's some of the easiest work, just repetitive and a little boring. Just do as you're told." Sebastian informs Tomas.

Sebastian hands Tomas some clean bandages and antibacterial cream. "Cover your brand with these bandages, but first dab on some of this antibacterial cream. There is less chance of infection if you keep the brand clean and covered."

"While we are working in the stables after we have finished with the work in the fields, I'll teach you how to feed, exercise, and care for the horses. I'll also explain what is expected of us later tonight."

"It'll be a long day. Do your best to keep up. Today is the day that we are given a few euros to shop with at the small gift shop for health and hygiene needs. I have a small stash of leftover euros from tips a few weeks ago. I'll show you where the gift shop is and help you get the things that we are allowed to buy for our own personal needs." Sebastian explains to Tomas.

"Merci, Sebastian."

Emmett and Francois clean up and return the breakfast plates to the indentured servant's kitchen. They take turns showering and go to bed. They will be allowed three to four hours of sleep before being expected to join in with the other workers in the fields and stables. Sebastian and Tomas exit the quarters. They walk side by side towards the fields. "Sebastian, you haven't told me how you ended up serving Monsieur Corbett?" Tomas inquires.

"Three years ago, I borrowed a large amount of money. Unable to pay my debts off, I came to Monsieur Corbett for a loan. Monsieur Corbett paid off my debts. I signed an ironclad contract. There's no way out. My debt to Monsieur Corbett never gets any smaller, only larger. Medical bills, room and board; we are charged for every drop of food and beverages we consume. It never ends. We're all in it for life.

You are only kidding yourself if you think you will ever pay off the debt owed to Monsieur Corbett."

"We'll be pulling weeds, mowing the grass, and tending to the grapes for the first half of the day. During the high heat of the day, we move into the stables, we exercise, feed and care for Monsieur Corbett's horses." Sebastian explains.

Days here can be long and hot. Water breaks are few and sparse. Emmett and Francois join Sebastian and Tomas in the stables later that afternoon. The day ends long after sunset. Evening meals are forgotten and replaced by private offering duties. There will be no rest, no sleep for Sebastian, Francois, Emmett, or Tomas.

Chapter 25

SEBASTIAN STUMBLES INTO THE SHOWER. FOR THE FIRST TIME IN eleven days, hot water cascades over his entire body. No cold showers tonight. Tomas steps into the shower next to Sebastian.

Sebastian turns and faces the wall, too embarrassed to allow Tomas to see him crying. Sebastian closes his eyes and takes a deep steadying breath struggling to compose himself. Tomas turns towards Sebastian, then gently places the palm of his hand on Sebastian's back. Sebastian flinches. "I'm sorry, I didn't mean to cause you pain. I've never… I mean... The lights, the cameras. I got nervous. I'm sorry." Tomas tries to explain.

"I don't blame you, it's not your fault. You were just doing as you were instructed. It's over. Our sacrifices tonight bought everyone a hot shower and six hours of uninterrupted sleep." Sebastian steps out of the shower and grabs a towel to dry off. He pulls on a clean pair of briefs.

Sebastian stares at his reflection in the mirror no longer recognizing his own reflection. Five years changes a man. He picks up his toothbrush and brushes his teeth. He turns towards the shower as he hears the water shut off and tosses a clean dry towel in Tomas' direction before walking out of the bathroom.

Sebastian lies down on his bed. Stretches out and closes his eyes.

For the first time in 72 hours Sebastian, Tomas, Emmett, and Francois are granted six precious hours of uninterrupted sleep.

Five long years. Twenty-one years of age. How much more could he endure? How much longer could his body hold up? How much longer would he survive?

Chapter 26

LUSCIOUS CORBETT POURS TWO GLASSES OF SCOTCH AND walks back to his desk. Corbett hands Dr. Roberts one glass and drinks from the second. He takes a seat behind his desk.

"Aaron, how long have we been friends?" Luscious asks.

"A long time. Over 20 years," Aaron Roberts answers.

"I know the reason for your visit. I know why you have traveled so far and what you have come to ask of me, but I'm afraid your trip has been made in vain. I'm afraid my answer has not changed. I'm sorry, my dear friend, the answer is still no." Luscious takes another sip of his scotch and waits for Aaron's response. Luscious knows that this particular conversation is far from over. In fact, it has only just begun.

"He no longer belongs in this world. He has paid his debt 10 times over. What possibly is left that the young man still owes you?" Aaron Roberts asks.

"He has accumulated a small fortune in medical bills that he has not yet paid back in full to the Chalet." Luscious swirls the scotch in his glass and takes another sip. "Honestly, what is your interest in this particular servant? What about this young man makes him any different from the others? Why is he more deserving of his freedom than any other servant at my Chalet? In over 20 years of friendship, you have never taken such a personal interest in any of the other personal offerings that you have counseled at my resort."

"I have provided you with 20 some years of service, Luscious. I have turned a blind eye to your illegal business practices. The use of indentured slaves for manual labor as well as perverted sexual labor. I have counseled many of those servants to better serve your Chalet. I have never spent any long period of personal time with one of your offerings until I met this particular young man. He has worked as my personal assistant as well as my personal chauffeur. I have gotten to know him on a more personal level than any other before him. He is educated, his services professional. I have gotten to know him better than any other doctor-patient relationship should have ever allowed. I will be the first to admit that was unprofessional of me. Happened all the same." Aaron Roberts informs his friend.

"As for the young man's medical debt, his injuries were caused by your son, Luc, and your nephew, Francois, while he was in service to your Chalet. As for his medical debt he has made you 10 times what you imagine he owes you.

I have never charged you for my services. I have never asked anything from you in return for my psychological counseling services. Luscious, just do right by this one young man. Grant me this one wish." Aaron implores of his old dear friend.

"What makes you think he would even accept an offer of freedom?"

"Why wouldn't he accept an offer of freedom, what would keep him from accepting what he has been working so hard to pay off?" Aaron Roberts asks.

"He has made friends. In the most unlikely of places, he has found a family. They have lost a few, had to bury the bodies of brothers and sisters they have learned to care about. They each have mourned their losses in their own ways. They look after and protect one another. He would never accept his freedom. He would never be able to leave his family behind. He is too honorable, too honest. That is why I can never set him free or sell his contract. He has been here for far too long. He knows too much about my business practices as well as my own personal habits," Luscious Corbett explains.

"Whose fault is that? You must see in him what I saw in him the first time I met him. The simple truth of the matter is that he scares you, Luscious. You fear the day will come when you will no longer be able to control him, no longer be able to silence him. He's a danger to you and your entire operation. How much longer will you be able to control him?"

"Fear him? No. He's been here for five years. For four of his five years he has worked off and on as a chauffeur/courier. He has never run. Every time he has left the grounds he has returned. He was involved in a car accident a few years back, totaled the Bentley. Never said one word to the police or EMTs who responded to the scene of the accident about who he worked for or about my personal business practices. He accepted blame for the accident that was in no way his fault. He accepted months of punishment fueled by my anger and rage. He never once begged for mercy. He silently accepted his daily punishments.

Honestly, I worry more about what to do with him after he's lost his sex appeal that has tripled my personal offerings requests since his arrival all those years ago. I will be forced to keep him busy with boring manual labor once he's lost his sex appeal." Luscious Corbett explains.

"Fear is what fuels him; fear is what drives his daily routine. By your own admittance. He didn't speak up when questioned by law enforcement out of fear. Your son, Luc, sat next to him and made sure of that.

It's not what torture he can't live through that drives him to remain silent, that forces him to return each time he leaves your Chalet. It's the knowledge and fear of the pain and torture that you will inflict upon his family that drives him to return each time he leaves. As long as he can protect them, he will. Loyalty to his family. Not to you or your precious Chalet. He will remain loyal as long as his family remains unharmed. You will purchase his absolute silence with their lives. Guarantee their safety and he is yours." Aaron Roberts defeatedly explains to Luscious.

"Just how, pray tell, do you propose I do that, Aaron?"

"I'm afraid the answer to that question is the one answer you don't really want to hear, the one truth you will never want to consider," Dr. Roberts sadly answers. His request lost in his own explanation.

11 Facts About Homeless Teens:

1) *39% of the homeless population is young people under the age of 18.*
2) *One in seven people between the ages of 10 to 18 will run away.*
3) *About 75% of homeless teens use drugs or alcohol as a means to self-medicate to deal with the traumatic experiences and abuse they face.*
4) *There are approximately 1.7 million homeless teens in the U.S.*
5) *5,000 young people die every year because of assault, illness, or suicide while on the streets.*
6) *A U.S. Department of Health and Human Services study found that 46% of homeless youth left their home because of physical abuse, 17% left because of sexual abuse.*
7) *Approximately 40% of homeless teens identify as LGBT.*
8) *Over 50% of young people in shelters and on the streets report that their parents told them to leave or knew they were leaving and didn't care.*
9) *The average age a teen becomes homeless is 14.7 years.*
10) *Teens ages 12-17 are more likely to become homeless than adults.*
11) *HIV rates for homeless young people are 2-10 times higher than reported rates for other samples of adolescents in the U.S.*

— *Do something.org*

The LGBTQ populace is trafficked too. Making people realize that whether or not they agree with homosexuality is trivial...Victimization and exploitation are the problem.

—- Nat Paul

Chapter 27

In all honesty, Sebastian's contract had been paid off in full by the end of his second year at the Chalet. Luscious Corbett hadn't lied when he'd told Aaron Roberts that Sebastian had tripled his business over the last five years. Sebastian's irresistible charm and rugged good looks, not to mention his young, muscular build, proved to be profitable among men and women visiting the Chalet over the last five years. Sebastian arrived at the Chalet all those years ago an inexperienced heterosexual virgin. Over the last five years he had learned to perform as an offering to both sexes without complaint.

He pleasures both men and women. Not always by his own personal choice but he always performs as instructed. He has learned his place and taken his lessons in stride. He has the strength to face his punishments in silence. If only the other servants were as strong as Sebastian.

His strong work ethic and sense of priority makes him irreplaceable in the stables and out in the fields. How could he sell or trade his contract to Aaron, no matter how far their friendship went back?

Aaron Roberts would purchase Sebastian's contract and set him free. That was a risk Luscious Corbett could not take.

Luscious swirls the last of his scotch, raises the glass to his mouth and swallows. He stands up, shuts off the desk lamp, and walks over to the corner office mini bar. He sits his glass down and turns to leave the office. Luscious Corbett stares down the barrel of his personally owned semi-automatic PAMAS G.

Broken, beaten, shattered, and scarred he stands facing his captor. Hands shaking, he presses the barrel of the PAMAS G into Monsieur Corbett's forehead. With every fiber of his being, he wants nothing more than to pull the trigger. Put an end to the brutal torture. Put an end to the humiliation, the pain, and the misery he's felt every day for the past five years at Luscious Corbett's Chalet.

The deafening shot rings out, the bullet enters Corbett's left temple. His body slumps to the floor. Hands shaking, ears ringing Sebastian drops the gun to the floor. It happened so fast. He doesn't even remember pulling the trigger. He falls to his knees and stares at his dead master's body lying on the carpet in a pool of blood. The shadow falling over him comes from the moonlit window behind him. Sebastian slowly turns and stands up he stares into Francois' pale face.

Francois slowly lowers his gun and drops it on the floor. They stare at one another both too scared to speak.

You never know how strong you are until being strong is your only choice.

—Bob Marley

Chapter 28

SEBASTIAN STANDS IN THE PROTECTION OF THE DARKENED tree line, he watches as Kindle walks past him along the path. The soft scent of vanilla floats on the air around her. He wants nothing more than to reach out, grab her up and never let go.

Sebastian refuses to endanger her life. If Luc ever found out about Kindle or her family he would not hesitate to torture and kill them.

Sebastian has been the property of Luc Corbett for eight long weeks. Luscious Corbett's death had changed nothing. Francois paid the ultimate price by pulling the trigger that night and killing his uncle. Sebastian had laid Francois' broken, shattered, beaten body to rest in the cold earth next to Sergei and the others. He had mourned his death forgiving his past. There was no more anger, no more hatred.

Francois had saved his life that night. He'd placed the PAMAS G in Sebastian's cold numb hands. He'd forced Sebastian out of the office that night, begged Sebastian to get rid of both guns. Following Francois' request he had buried both guns with Francois' body six feet deep in the cold, dark earth.

He had not seen or spoken to Dr. Aaron Roberts since the fateful night Dr. Roberts had placed the PAMAS G in his hands.

Nothing had changed, it was no worse as feared, but it was no better. Life went on. Sebastian fed and groomed the horses, he drove clients and delivered packages. He was still a popular offering most nights. He guarded and protected his family. But most of all, he loved Kindle. It was time to let go of her. It was time to set her free. Sebastian could no longer protect his family. The disease consumed his body, weakening him. He didn't have long. His life was ending. His fight was over. There was nothing that could be done for him. Kindle deserved better; she deserved a life.

Kindle opens the letter box; the soft scent of peppermint oil fills the air. She smiles and reaches into the box to remove his letter. Sebastian watches as she turns and walks back by him. The soft scent of peppermint and vanilla floats on the air. Kindle tears the letter open and pulls out the single sheet of paper. As she approaches the front patio where her mother and father await her return, she collapses to the ground. Christian Raines rushes to his daughter's side. He embraces her and stares at the simple words printed on a single sheet of paper lying on the ground next to his daughter. Jenna gasps and collapses into tears next to her daughter.

> Broken, Beaten, Battered and Bruised… Fractured Souls, Shattered Dreams.
> Through it all my heart still beats, your precious memories kept me alive.
> My Dearest Kindle, I set you free….
> My Dearest Kindle, I die free….

Unable to breath, unable to watch any longer, Sebastian inhales one last breath of peppermint oil and vanilla. Tears in his eyes and an ache in his chest he quietly turns and walks back to the car. With one last glance he drives away refusing to look back. For just one single moment he wonders how far he could get before the tank runs out of gas. How far he could get on foot after that. How long it would take Luc to find him and string him up, beat him till there was nothing left to shatter or break. He knows what he must do, he knows it's the only way out. It's the only choice he has left. He pulls the Bentley over and parks on the side of the road two kilometers from the Raines farm, a road he knows Inspector Raines drives daily on his way to work. He places the map on the seat next to him. He's carefully marked and named each of their graves, he sits the stationary from the Chalet with the names of his extended family, every last one of them next to the map. His final act of protection. He would set them all free.

Sebastian's heart aches. Pain and misery consume him. His memory is full of a world he never should have known. So many lives shattered. The GPS monitor on his left wrist reminds him what he must do, it's the only way. He has been off course for too long, Luc is bound to take notice. Sebastian reaches up and activates the Navigational GPS Emergency Services Beacon. He reaches into the glove box and removes a small package, he tears it open. He's done everything he can think of to protect his ever growing family.

The needle enters his arm. He pushes it deep into his vain. Slowly he pushes the plunger. Dr. Nairobi Adeel Maboob's final gift takes immediate effect. With his last breath he softly whispers her name one last time. "*Kindle.*"

Brisé, battu, battues et meurtri. Des âmes fracturées, des rêves brisés.
À travers tout mon coeur bat encore, vos précieux souvenirs m'ont gardé en vie.
Mon très cher Kindle, je vous ai mis gratuitement....
Mon très cher Kindle, je meurs libre....

Broken, Beaten, Battered and Bruised. Fractured souls. Shattered dreams.
Through it all my heart still beats, your precious memories kept me alive.
My dearest Kindle, I set you free....
My dearest Kindle, I die free....

First and foremost, I wish to thank my husband for his endless patience, love and support as I sat up sleepless night after sleepless night researching Human Trafficking and writing till all hours of the night and morning. Gj you will always be my greatest strength.

My family and friends for their endless support.

I wish to thank the brave young men and women who relived the worst moments of their lives. Who shared with me their horrors and worst nightmares to help spread awareness and to help educate the public.

Last, but certainly not least, I wish to thank everyone who took the time to read my letters of inquiry and answer my questions with brutal honesty. I quoted a few and included as many brutal truthful facts as possible.

God bless all of you, an author is only as strong as those who support their work.

CPSIA information can be obtained
at www.ICGtesting.com
Printed in the USA
LVHW080155100422
715792LV00010B/703

9 781636 611174